SECRETS
AND
LIES

Gina Amos

Secrets and Lies
Gina Amos
Copyright © 2014 Kara Group Pty Limited

PO Box 277
Hunters Hill NSW 2110 Australia
ht@kara.com.au

ISBN 978-0-9923105-4-7
Kara Group Pty Limited
PO Box 277
Hunters Hill NSW 2110 Australia
ht@kara.com.au
First published 2011

For Mark, Zoe and Alex

*Pride goeth before a fall and
haughty spirit before destruction*
(Proverbs16.18)

It was autumn, the season of change. The sun was shining but a distinct chill permeated the air. The deciduous trees put on a colourful display and the russet and mustard coloured leaves formed a backdrop to what was normally an average suburban street. Over time, the trees would be stripped bare, the streetscape would change and the leaves would clog the gutters and block the drains. They would become a nuisance, an inconvenience.

Chapter One

The walk home had seemed longer today, her throat was dry, her spirits low. Astrid, sauntered out from a crack in the laundry door and flaunted her tail in the air as she rubbed herself up against Rose's leg. The old woman smiled, bent over and fondled the cat's chin, scolding her softly as she reached up for the china teapot on the shelf above the range-hood. The painted portrait of a young Elizabeth II etched upon the teapot had faded, her nose was missing and the gold trim around the handle had worn away. Rose shook her head as an acceptance that nothing lasts forever, threw a handful of tea leaves into the pot and lit the gas hob with a match. As she waited for the kettle to boil she realised that it had only been a week since Suellyn had told her that she was selling the house and the thought of that day haunted her still. It was a Tuesday; it was the day she had made the mistake of opening the door to her daughter-in-law. It had been raining...

It was raining. Heavy, wet drops splashed against the verandah steps.

'Oh, it's only you, Suellyn,' Rose said, as she stepped back from the screen door. 'Come in out of the rain for goodness sake. I wasn't expecting to see you so soon, especially on a day like today.'

'You know I like to keep an eye on you, Rose, to see if you're managing.' Suellyn shook the rain from her umbrella, wiped her shoes on the 'welcome' mat and followed Rose into the kitchen. She sat down at the kitchen table in an uncomfortable, high back chair and watched as she filled the kettle until it overflowed.

'I know it's here somewhere,' she said, annoyed by her own absent-mindedness. Rose searched the cupboards for the caddy filled with Earl Grey tea, Suellyn looked around her at the state of the kitchen and wondered how Rose could live like this and wondered whether it bothered her.

'Ah, here it is,' Rose said, as if she had just found something of great value. 'You don't mind if I have a cuppa do you dear?' Suellyn didn't drink tea, she didn't like the bitter taste or the drawn out ritual that tea drinking involved. Rose reached into the biscuit barrel and carefully laid out four iced biscuits on a small, round plate.

For the past two months, Suellyn Phillips had tried everything she could think of to persuade her mother-in-law to move from the house in Eden Street to a unit in a nearby retirement village. But Rose was determined to stay where she was. There was Astrid to consider and Rose knew her feline friend would not be welcome at the Bayside Retirement Village.

Max Gray lived around the corner in Dalgetty Street and arrived on her doorstep at nine am sharp on the first day of every month, regular as clockwork, just as he had done for the past eight years. Despite his surname, Max was outgoing and friendly. The sweat-stained hat he wore to protect himself from the weather was too large for his head and a red V from too much time spent in the sun was visible from his opened necked shirt. His monthly visits were a welcome diversion to Rose's lonely life and she looked forward to their conversations over a cup of tea before he headed out to work in her garden. Rose enjoyed listening to the descriptions of his family's get-togethers, of twenty first birthday parties, weddings, christenings and his recent eightieth birthday celebration at the local bowling club, which she had been invited to, but did not attend.

Suellyn stood by the kitchen sink and gazed out the grimy window. She was watching Max Gray as he emptied a bag of weeds into the compost bin and was thinking of how she would tell Rose. She would choose her words carefully she decided. She turned away from the window and poured the tea, added three heaped teaspoons of sugar and a slip of milk. It was just the way Rose liked it, hot and sweet. Rose lifted the cup from the saucer and placed it on the table. She poured a small measure of tea into the saucer and blew on it before she brought it to her lips and slurped. This annoyed her daughter-in-law and perhaps that's why she did it.

'I might as well tell you now,' Suellyn said, as she picked up the teapot and refilled Rose's cup. She waited a moment, looked at her mother-in-law and set down the teapot firmly on the tea stand. Rose raised her eyes and looked at Suellyn squarely, noticing the tightness of her daughter-in-law's lips.

'Rose,' she said and paused again, hoping to gain her full attention. When she was sure she had it, she continued. 'I've decided. I'm not going to waste any-more time talking about it, I'm selling the house.'

'Whose house Suellyn, dear?' Rose asked, as she placed the saucer on the table and looked expectantly at Suellyn.

'Why, this house of course.'

'Don't be silly.'

'I'm serious Rose. I've spoken to a real estate agent. Her name's Ambah St John. Here's her business card.' Suellyn pushed the card across the table. Rose picked up the glossy, matchbox sized card and studied it. She couldn't read the name on it; she needed her reading glasses for that.

'Ambah works for the real estate agency in the village, the one next to the bank on the corner, near the traffic lights.' Suellyn was speaking quickly now and Rose was having trouble following her. Suellyn was firing words at her like a Gatling gun, trying to get them out quickly, so she could say what she had to say and leave.

'You might as well know I've put down a deposit on a unit at the retirement village. The one we've talked about. You'll be more comfortable there Rose, you know you will if you're honest with yourself. Let's face it - it has to be a damn sight better than all of this.' Suellyn raised her arms and swung them around in a wide arc.

Rose didn't follow Suellyn's gestures; instead, she poured more tea and placed both hands around the teacup to warm them. Rose suddenly felt cold and shuddered when she noticed a fine hairline crack which ran the length of the cup. Soft rose pink in colour, it was from her favourite set. It reminded her of another day, of a day long ago and of another conversation in a café in the city with her son, Billy. Overcome with sadness, regret and a sense of dread, she wondered why Suellyn wanted to sell the house.

'Are you listening to me Rose? Do you understand what I am saying to you?'

'I'm not deaf and I'm not stupid. This is my home and I've told you before, I don't want to go anywhere. I'm happy living here and besides, what will happen to Astrid?'

'Forget about the damn cat will you? Christ, you're a stubborn woman Rose Phillips. Just remember, this house is in my name and if I want to sell it, I will. Anyway, it's too late now, I've already made an appointment with Ambah. She said she's going to drop by sometime next week to inspect the house. And Rose, I expect you to co-operate with her.'

'Does Billy know about this?' Rose asked. 'Does he know that you want to throw me out onto the street?' She demanded to know if Billy knew what his wife was planning. Rose looked down at the muddied tea and the dark shadow of tea leaves which were sitting at the bottom of the teacup.

'He'll know soon enough and I'm not throwing

you out onto the street. Haven't you heard a single word I've said?'

Rose raised her head slowly and looked at her daughter-in-law. 'I heard you well enough Suellyn, and you might want to listen to me for once. The only way I'm leaving this house is in a pine box, so go tell that to Billy.'

Suellyn stared at Rose's determined face and expelled a long, loud sigh. Rose folded her arms across her hollow chest and stared back at her daughter-in-law. Nothing more was said, there was nothing more *to* say. Suellyn placed her hands on the table, leaned forward and looked into Rose's watery eyes before turning away when she saw the cold determination in them. In defiance, Rose took a large bite from an iced biscuit and sipped her tea which was now tepid. Suellyn grabbed her handbag and stormed out of the house.

The front door snapped shut. Rose studied her swollen fingers as she placed her cup back on the saucer and reflected, not for the first time, on her son's taste in women. Grim-faced, Rose thought about what Suellyn had just said to her. She knew her daughter-in-law and knew what she was capable of. The next time they met, she would have the real estate agent with her. But Rose didn't see Suellyn again and she never did discover the reason why she wanted her out of the house.

Suellyn grabbed her umbrella and stepped off the verandah onto the brick path which led to the front gate. She turned and looked over her shoulder, towards the neighbour's hedge which was covered in clouds of white flowers and purple berries. The clicking sound of garden clippers suddenly stopped. He was standing there, quietly watching her. The sweet smell of cut branches and scented flowers drifted towards her and she spotted Rose's neighbour behind the collapsed timber fence. Suellyn tried to recall his name then turned her back on him and walked quickly out through the gate and towards her parked car.

Chapter Two

It wasn't unusual for the traffic to be heavy on Military Road and today was no different from any other. Suellyn's foot slipped on the accelerator and to compensate she braked hard, narrowly missing the car ahead. Her breathing was shallow and laboured. She clenched her teeth when she spotted the amber traffic light ahead. She didn't care if the red light camera caught her, the loss of points on her licence and the fine didn't bother her either, she just wanted to get home before she changed her mind.

The light turned red before she made it through the intersection and a learner driver in a yellow Suzuki hatchback made an insane right hand turn in front of her into a one-way street. Suellyn punched heavily on the horn and changed lanes in time to avoid the Suzuki and changed back again to avoid hitting a delivery van parked in a loading zone.

It was a slow drive home but eventually the familiar row of Manly Pines appeared ahead and marked the entrance to her apartment block. Suellyn sighed with relief as she flicked the indicator and drove down into the basement car park, braking hard at the vehicle barrier gate as she gripped the steering wheel and stared out through the windscreen, waiting for the mechanical arm to lift. The rubber tyres slipped and squealed on the polished concrete floor as she turned and parked in bay number sixteen. The car door slammed and echoed through the empty car park. Instead of taking the stairs to their eighth floor apartment, as she usually did, she pressed the button on the lift panel and waited for it to arrive.

The Panorama was an eight storey residential building located at the southern end of Manly Beach. The Phillips's apartment faced east and looked out across the ocean. There were two apartments to each floor and a French executive occupied the neighbouring apartment. He used it for entertaining clients when he was in town. Jean-Claude Broussard was in his forties and was fat and bald. His name was all that Suellyn had found attractive about him and the pair had got no further than their initial introductions after they had stood together one morning in the corridor, waiting for a lift to take them down to the basement car park.

Suellyn quickly unlocked the apartment door and in her haste, she tripped on the thick Persian rug in the hallway. She hissed as she kicked off her heels and ran barefoot into the study. The room was dark and instinctively she grabbed the damask curtains and yanked them back. They parted and revealed a sparkling, million dollar view, but she wasn't interested in the view today, she had more important things on her mind. Law books and files were littered on William's desk. She pushed them aside, sat down in his chair and pulled herself up to the edge of the desk. She hit the computer keyboard and the iMac sprang back from a deep sleep, responding to her demands, sensing her impatience. The Internet quickly connected and Suellyn found the website she had been looking for - Energex's six digit telephone enquiry number flashed onto the screen in front of her. She hammered the number into the phone and wedged the handset between her neck and shoulder. It seemed more like hours than minutes before the operator finally answered.

'Yes, good morning. I want to disconnect the power at my rental property. It's vacant, there's nobody living there.'

The operator recorded the details and asked Suellyn to hold. Meanwhile, Suellyn looked out through the window at the ocean which was calm and unruffled, exactly the opposite to the way she was feeling. A red and yellow Surf Rescue helicopter came into view and flew low over the coastline like some gigantic, flying wasp, flapping its wings above its head. The chopper was about one hundred metres from the shore and the sound of the deep thwap, thwap of the helicopter's blades distracted her for a moment as she watched it bank sharply to the right and head back out to sea.

The operator came back on the line, prompting Suellyn to uncross her shapely legs and sit upright.

'Yes, that's right, 15 Eden Street. You can send the final invoice to my private post office box.'

As Suellyn hung up, she felt strangely satisfied even though her stomach felt like a dozen butterflies were performing back flips. She was convinced that everyone would be better off and Rose would come to realise that it was in her best interests to move to the retirement village. Besides, Rose had no other choice did she? Suellyn was sure she would come to her senses and realise that she was deadly serious about selling the house.

The thought suddenly crossed Suellyn's mind that Rose might decide to stay in the house just to spite her and if that was the case, she wondered what else she could do to persuade her to leave. Other options came to mind, but the next thing on her list was to sack Max Gray, the gardener. He and Rose were far too cosy. If he found out that the power had been disconnected he might want to do something about it; he might want to help her in some way.

It was stale and airless inside the apartment and as Suellyn slid open the glass doors, she began to relax with the sound of the waves and the briny smell of the ocean as it drifted across the terrace and into the apartment.

The lounge-room opened out onto a spacious limestone terrace and the bank of white nylon curtains shivered and floated into the room like billowing sails. The movement of the curtains as they shifted about and licked at a potted indoor palm, helped to calm her nerves. She collapsed onto the white leather lounge and propped her head up against a cushion. She took a deep breath and a quiver of a smile broke out across her face as she rolled over onto her side. Her chestnut coloured hair fell in perfect waves against the nape of her neck. The cordless phone was within her reach and she grabbed at it and dialed Tommy Dwyer's home phone number. He answered immediately as if he had been expecting her call.

'Hi, it's me. I'm just about to leave.'

'I was wondering when you were going to call. What have you been up to? I can hear the excitement in your voice.'

'You'll be so proud of me Tommy. I've finally worked out a way of getting Rose to move out of the house.'

'Well, go on then, tell me, don't keep me in suspense.' Tommy held the phone hard up against his ear and concentrated.

'I've already spoken to a real estate agent. She said she can call around next week to inspect the house.'

A large grin broke out across his lips; a dimple creased his left cheek. 'I can't wait for you to get here so you can tell me all about it. Make sure you drive carefully, you know you always drive too fast on the freeway and the road will be slippery after all the rain.' Tommy put the phone down and returned to the article in the *Medical Journal of Australia*. He leant over and pushed down heavily on the stainless steel coffee plunger and poured himself another cup of strong coffee. It was lukewarm. He drained the cup, looked at his watch and calculated Suellyn would arrive after lunch. Tommy stood up from the lounge, stretched his arms above his head, yawned and threw the magazine into the fireplace. It slowly disappeared into the dying embers without a trace.

Chapter Three

The sun broke through the grey clouds as Suel-lyn drove into the busy petrol station on Dunbar Street. She filled the Porsche with enough petrol for the return trip and as she waited in line to pay, she checked her phone for messages. At the head of the queue she pulled out her credit card, gave the cashier a sour look and told him to charge her for the chocolate bar and a bottle of pomegranate juice she intended to grab on her way out.

As she took the exit ramp onto the freeway, every nervous fibre in her body began to relax. She eased her head back onto the leather headrest and as the CD began to play, angry images of her mother-in-law slowly began to disappear. She had expected Rose to agree to move when she'd told her she'd already put down a deposit on the unit at the retirement village this morning. But Rose seemed more determined than ever to stay where she was and because of that, she was going to suffer. It served her right for being so stubborn she thought, as she settled back into the rhythm of the freeway.

It was a two hour drive to the beach house and she put her foot down when she spotted the 110km speed sign ahead. Suellyn loved the Porsche and found the speed and power of the vehicle exhilarating. As she sped down the freeway and passed the traffic on her left, she felt strangely satisfied. For the first time in her married life, she suddenly felt she was in control.

A *Cold Chisel* CD was playing and she turned the volume up loud when her favourite track began to play. The air-con was set at a comfortable twenty-two degrees and her body felt cocooned and safe. She was glad to be leaving the traffic and the bustling confusion of the city behind. The weather was clear and being a weekday, there wasn't much traffic about apart from a few transporters heading north, exceeding the speed limit, trying to meet their unrealistic deadlines. Suellyn made a sharp exit at the turn-off to Tommy's house and as she drove along the deserted gravel road she was suddenly reminded of why she loved it here, especially during autumn. The air was clean, her mind was more settled and she could stretch her eyes towards the horizon. There were solitary walks to the headland to look forward to while Tommy was content to sit in front of the open fire, lost to a book and a bottle of red wine.

The beach house was designed to take advantage of the water views and the surrounding coastal habitat. The sandy soil was perfect for growing Australian native plants and the heath banksias and grevilleas Tommy had planted thrived and attracted lorikeets and king parrots which appeared at sunrise and sunset to feast on the sweet nectar. Tommy loved gardening, a hobby which he had shared with his father, but Suellyn didn't care much for his passion. It was too much like hard work for her liking. A makeshift wire fence was all that separated the garden from the beach.

Pebble Beach was a tranquil and safe place to swim. North facing, it was visited by families with young children who enjoyed the beach with its thin line of creamy coloured sand and gentle waves. It was quiet at this time of year apart from the occasional retired couple who could be seen walking along the shoreline and the small groups of mothers, who with their determined faced toddlers splashed in the shallows; the children armed with brightly coloured plastic buckets and spades.

Suellyn loved the beach house. She loved lying in bed with Tommy late at night and also before the pale dawn when she couldn't sleep, looking out the bedroom window, watching the waves as they gently caressed the beach, watching for the sun to make its appearance and always feeling safe in Tommy's arms.

He told her the beach house would be hers if she married him, promising he would transfer the title to her. The idea of owning the beach house, appealed to Suellyn, but she wasn't so sure about his marriage proposal - she already had a husband. But she wasn't thinking about that just yet. It was enough for her to be with him. Life wasn't complicated with Tommy Dwyer and the thirty year age gap didn't bother her either. Tommy at sixty-four, was more like a father to her than a lover, and she didn't have a problem with that. Spoiling her and treating her like a princess was how he had managed to weave himself into her life.

The tyres crunched on the gravel driveway and came to an abrupt stop in front of the house, firing bursts of gravel in all directions. The driver's door swung open and Suellyn's tanned, shapely legs planted themselves firmly on the ground. A green and red parrot swooped down to greet her, she squealed and ducked as it flew off towards the beach.

'Sues!'

Suellyn smiled and laughed at Tommy as he attempted a lighthearted skip down the timber steps to greet her. He ran one hand through his hair and grabbed her overnight bag with the other. He kissed her long and hard on the mouth and pressed himself into her.

Suellyn released herself from his grip and stared at him with a *not now* look.

'I can't wait to get changed,' she said, as she grabbed her bag back from him and pulled open the screen door. 'Great weather. I love this time of year, don't you Tommy?' she called to him from the bedroom. She dumped her opened overnight bag on the floor. Her clothes formed a pile in one corner of the room and the contents of her handbag spewed out onto the bed. She released her feet from her uncomfortable high heels and replaced them with a sensible pair of sandals. 'Are you coming Tommy?' she called out as she pulled up her tracksuit pants and tied a knot at the waist.

'No, you go, I'll get dinner started.'

Suellyn quietly slipped out of the back door with a towel and a book under her arm. The hazy autumn sunshine warmed her body. Without a trace of cloud or hint of a sea breeze, Suellyn soon found herself day-dreaming as she sat staring out at the gentle movement of the ocean. She felt part of its rhythm, unrelenting, unforgiving; lost in thought she gazed at the distant horizon through wrap around sunglasses. The breeze tainted with the smell of the sea gently drifted towards her, across the empty expanse of the ocean, coated with memories. Memories of family holidays catching small fish in nets, racing home to proudly show her father, then leaving them in a plastic bucket by the back door to slowly suffocate, while she went off to play with her cousins on the sandy dunes.

It was late afternoon, the sun was thinking about setting when the back screen door opened. Tommy removed his reading glasses and listened as Suellyn's footsteps hit the timber floorboards.

'How was the beach?' Tommy asked, as she collapsed next to him on the bulky sofa in front of the fireplace. Suellyn hugged herself and brought her feet up onto the lounge. The crackling fire warmed the chill from her bones and cast its warmth and light into the room.

'Peaceful. I'm so relaxed, the tension just disappears when I'm here. Must be something to do with the salt air.'

'I thought you were going to say it had something to do with being with me.'

She smiled back at him, feeling guilty, sensing that his feelings were hurt. She leant into him and pinched his cheek and watched as a dimple formed.

'So, tell me Sues what have you been up to? You got something on your mind you want to unload?'

Tommy Dwyer was the only person to ever call Suellyn, Sues. She loved the familiarity and casualness between them and as she shrugged her shoulders, she grabbed the soft, check mohair blanket from the back of the sofa, wrapped it around her and nuzzled into him. He couldn't understand why she was playing with him, why she just didn't come out and tell him what she had done to persuade Rose to move out of the house. He arched his eyebrows and waited patiently for an answer to his question. But there was none. There was no use pressing the point. Tommy knew Suellyn Phillips only too well, she would tell him what she had been up to in her own good time.

The next morning, Tommy filled the cafetière with the ground coffee beans he had bought from an organic farm on the outskirts of Byron Bay and watched as the mist above the waves rolled in towards the beach. He knew Suellyn would have to go back to the city after lunch. They had to talk. They had to go over the plan again. He had to be sure that Rose's house would sell but he had decided to wait until she was up and showered before talking to her.

'I'm going to the shops to get a few things. Do you want me to get you anything special from the deli?' he called out from the kitchen.

'No.' Suellyn groaned. She was still in bed, her head thick from too much wine the night before.

'Where are your car keys?'

'Coffee table, lounge-room,' she replied.

'Got them, won't be long. I'll bring something back for lunch.'

Half an hour after Tommy left, Suellyn yawned

openly, rolled over onto her side and looked at the display of red numbers on the clock radio. It was ten-thirty. Her stomach rumbled and she needed to go to the bathroom. The mirrored wardrobe was ajar and as she examined her reflection in the mirror, she saw the silk robe hanging amongst Tommy's clothes. She threw back the covers and swung her legs over the side of the bed. She slid the glass door open. The robe slipped from the timber coat hanger and fell to the floor. She picked it up, pulled it on and wrapped it around her body. She was surprised to find it was a perfect fit. The raw silk against her naked body felt soft, cool, and luxurious and as she looked into the mirror, she moistened her lips, tightened the belt around her narrow waist then turned away and walked into the bathroom.

Suellyn had been drawn to Tommy Dwyer out of loneliness and longing. From the moment she looked into his eyes she felt a connection. Their relationship began with a chance meeting at a bar in the city. After turning up for Friday night drinks with friends, she spotted him. He was propped up at the bar with a glass of red wine, tapping his fingers gently in time to the music. He was well dressed in a dark jacket, white shirt and a neatly knotted tie. Suellyn had instantly liked what she saw. He had the darkest eyes she had ever seen, thin sensuous lips and a dimple which creased his cheek when he smiled. Even though he appeared to be in his sixties, she was immediately drawn to him and in hindsight, his likeness to William was probably why she was attracted to him.

Suellyn Phillips had always preferred older men,

they knew how women liked to be treated. He was ten years older than William and surprisingly he was an only child, as was William. The first thing he told her was that his mother had recently died and Suellyn felt sorry for him. From his description of her, they had obviously been close.

'What did you buy?' Suellyn asked as Tommy flung the plastic shopping bags across the bench and looked at her standing in the kitchen doorway.

'I see you found the robe. I was going to surprise you with it; it belonged to my mother. Suellyn fondled the silk with her fingers and loosened the belt, it fell away easily, her eyes glinted, her chest rose and she held her breath.

Chapter Four

It was nine am. Ambah St John inspected her makeup in the mirror on the back of the sun visor before she stepped out of the car and walked towards the front gate of the dilapidated house. Her client, Suellyn Phillips, had phoned and said she couldn't meet her this morning, something unexpected had come up, but she assured her that her mother-in-law would be at home and would be expecting her.

The steel gate groaned as she pushed against it. A rusty hinge came away and landed on the ground in front of her and Ambah made a mental note to mention it to Suellyn the next time they met. After all, first impressions were important, especially in a buyer's market. Ambah carefully closed the front gate behind her and walked along the brick path and across the verandah towards the front door. She knocked twice and waited, allowing enough time for the elderly woman to answer her knock. She knocked again but realised that the woman she had come to see didn't seem to be at home. She was annoyed. Suellyn had assured her that the old woman would be expecting her.

Rose Phillips was elderly and Ambah knew that most elderly people were early risers and most were forgetful. She was reminded of her own grandmother. Nana Rey was up and dressed and having her first cup of tea of the day by five every morning and in bed by six every evening. Ambah checked her watch and wondered if she should come back later, but she had a full day of appointments scheduled and this was the only opportunity this week she would have to inspect the house. She knew how anxious her client was to have the marketing campaign underway.

She knocked again, this time a little louder. Still, there was no answer. From somewhere inside the house a cat whined. Ambah stood on the front steps and looked out at the street to check if any of the neighbours were watching before she made her way to the side of the house. She walked down the narrow side passage taking care not to scratch her black patent heels or snag her stockings. She walked on tiptoes through the overgrown weeds, sidestepped the empty paint tins, broken bricks and the plastic crates filled with empty beer bottles.

Suellyn had given her a set of house plans and she had carefully studied them before leaving the office and now as she stood beside the house, she was annoyed with herself that she'd not thought to ask for a set of house keys as well. She couldn't contact the old woman by phone to confirm their meeting – according to Suellyn, the phone had been disconnected years ago.

Ambah raised her head and looked up. The kitchen window looked out across the next-door neighbour's yard and she recognised that the leafy outlook would be a good selling point. From what she had seen so far, the property had potential, but she was eager to discover how the inside of the house presented.

An empty, plastic milk crate lay on its side, propped up against a wheelbarrow filled with damp leaf litter which had fallen from the neighbour's gum tree. She turned the crate on its end and pushed it down into the soft grass with her foot, stepped on it and dug her toes deep into the narrow points of her shoes. She slung her handbag over her shoulder and criss-crossed it against her body so it rested comfortably on her hip. Bracing herself against the brick wall of the house she stretched her body to its full height, a petite one hundred and sixty-four centimetres. Loose, paper-thin flakes of green paint from the window casement came away in her hands.

Ambah tried to imagine what she would do if the old woman was at home after all and caught her peering through the kitchen window. How ridiculous she would seem.

The windows were thick with dust. A layer of grime and lacy cobwebs covered the glass. A spider with a small, black body and long, hairy legs scurried across the pane and lodged itself in the corner of the window sill. Ambah watched it for a moment from the corner of her eye, keeping her distance, before she turned and cupped her hands against the glass pane. She narrowed her eyes and screwed them tightly, her eyebrows flexed as she tried to distinguish the features inside the room, but the morning sun made it difficult to make sense of the scene before her. As her eyes focused, a raw, primitive scream clawed its way up from the back of her throat, exploded and cut through the silence like a knife through a block of butter. Her eyes widened. This was the last thing she had expected, nothing she had ever done or seen before had prepared her for this.

'Oh my God!' Ambah's face brushed against the window, trying to make sense of what she was seeing.

A hip-hop ring tone pierced the silence. Beads of perspiration had already formed on her forehead, a strand of bleached hair fell across her eyes and her heart thumped as her pulse climbed. She unzipped her handbag and grabbed her phone with both hands. The caller ID read 'Mum'. She answered it. 'I can't talk now Mum, got an emergency. I'll ring you back.'

'Ambah, what's the matter? I...' her mother called down the phone. Ambah pushed the 'end call' button and punched 000 into the phone. With shaking hands, and legs that felt like jelly, she tried to keep her balance on the crate as she spoke to the emergency operator. She took a deep breath, silently reminding herself it was important that she remained calm. She was trying to sound as if she had control of the situation, but it was no use. Her speech was halted, she was breathless, agitated. '...15 Eden Street and please, please hurry,' she heard herself say before the milk crate slipped from underneath her. She fell to the ground, landing on her knees. She rolled over into a sitting position and pressed her back hard up against the brick wall of the house. Grabbing her knees, she brought them up to her chest and touched her cheek with the palm of her hand. Her cheek was hot and sticky with blood.

Sirens screamed in the distance. But Ambah knew she had to take another look before the police and the ambulance arrived, if only to convince herself of what she had seen. She kicked off her shoes and stepped back onto the crate. She did not want to lose her balance this time and wedged the crate firmly against the house. She grabbed the window-ledge tightly with her sweaty palms and looked again through the window at the lifeless body of the woman she assumed was Rose Phillips. The woman's head lolled to one side, her arms hung loosely over the side of the kitchen chair at an awkward angle.

Ambah had never seen a dead body before; she was still young enough not to have been affected by death. She was repulsed by the greenish-red tinge of the woman's flesh. She bit down heavily on her lower lip and tasted her own salty blood.

The sirens were close now. Ambah stepped off the crate and pushed her feet back into her shoes and made her way around to the front of the house. She ran her hands through her long hair and straightened her skirt.

'Over here!' Ambah called out to two police officers as they walked towards the front gate. Jill Brennan and her partner pulled on their black leather gloves.

'Hello. I'm Senior Constable Brennan and this is Constable French. And you are?'

Ambah gave her full name and a brief description of what she had seen before leading the officers down the side of the house.

Ambah and Brennan stood back and watched as Daniel French stood on his toes and looked through the window. He was lanky, somewhat awkward and she estimated that he was at least one hundred and ninety centimetres tall. Jill Brennan on the other hand, was short and petite but had an air of confidence and maturity about her that Ambah recognised in herself and other women of her generation. She looked like she didn't take crap from anyone.

The morning sun was bouncing off the filthy window, throwing shadows back at him. The young police constable cupped his hands against the window pane just as Ambah had done ten minutes earlier and he saw the old woman's body slumped against the kitchen table. Jill joined her partner and climbed onto the milk crate and stood next to him, balancing herself on one leg with her arm resting on his shoulder.

'We're going to have to cordon off the front of the house with tape and while you're at it Dan, call in another police truck - we're going to need some assistance here to protect the scene.'

'I'll have to ask you to remain outside,' Brennan said to Ambah as she opened the screen door and pushed her shoulder against the front door which was unlocked. As Brennan made her way down the hall towards the kitchen, the two paramedics took their cue from her, and followed close behind. Jill Brennan had a feeling that this wasn't going to be a good day, and she was right, they all smelt Rose Phillips before they saw her.

'No need to resuc,' someone joked. Jill covered her mouth and nose with the back of her hand.

Rose had not finished the cup of tea she had been drinking. A thick film of grey mould floated on the surface of the liquid and the silence in the room was interrupted only by the persistent buzzing of flies. Ants had eaten the crumbed remains of an iced biscuit and the woollen coat Rose was wearing smelt of mothballs. Two empty packets of pills lay on the table. A sleek, grey cat sneaked out from the laundry, jumped onto the kitchen table and turned up its nose at the remainder of the mouldy tea in the cup.

'Shit, what a mess.' The paramedics covered their faces with masks.

'Got any idea what's happened here?' Brennan asked the more senior of the two. The name tag on his uniform said Cooke; he looked vaguely familiar.

'Hard to say. I'm no expert, but by the look and smell of her, she's probably been dead for a couple of days. Turn the light on will you fellas? It's so dark in here we can't see what we're bloody well doing.'

Brennan flicked the light on in the kitchen. She flicked the switch again. On, off, on, off.

The police truck door was wide open. French was leaning inside to grab the roll of blue and white crime scene tape from the back seat when Detective Senior Sergeant Rimis approached the truck.

'What's happened here Constable?'

French spun around and faced his superior. Rimis flashed his ID.

'An old woman dead, Sarge. Senior Constable Brennan's inside.'

Rimis nodded stiffly and instead of going inside, he walked off in the direction of the next door neighbour's house.

'The lights aren't working. Check the power will you, Dan?' Daniel French was on the front verandah about to walk back inside when he heard Brennan call out to him. He checked the power board on the wall next to the door.

'Looks all okay, the circuit breaker hasn't tripped, maybe the power's been disconnected.' He closed the screen door behind him and walked into the kitchen to join his partner. 'Better watch what you say, there's a Detective Senior Sergeant snooping around outside. I don't know what he's doing here but he's gone to talk to the next-door neighbour.'

Jill nodded and tightened her short ponytail with her fingers. 'Dan, can you check with all the electricity suppliers, find out what's going on with the power, and while you're at it, go back out to the truck and grab a couple of torches. It's so dark in here. I'll take a look through her belongings for some ID and any details of the next of kin.'

'I can give you the details of the next of kin, officer.' Ambah St John emerged from the dark shadows of the lounge-room. 'The woman is the mother-in-law of my client. I've got her details and a business contact address for Mr Phillips, Rose Phillip's son, here,' Ambah said, as she tapped her phone and handed Brennan her business card.

Brennan took the card and studied the real estate agent standing in front of her. She was a young, attractive, peroxide blonde, and her left ear was missing an earring. Her black stockings were laddered and a thin line of red lipstick smudged the side of her mouth. Limp strands of hair fell across her face, her cheek was grazed and the dried blood on her face gave her the appearance of a street kid. Jill had seen plenty of those since joining the force, especially on the night shift up at the Cross.

Brennan looked at the pen and pocket-sized spiral note pad in Ambah's hand. It was obvious she was taking advantage of a bad situation. She had been poking around the house, taking an inventory. Brennan didn't feel sorry for the young woman standing in front of her anymore. More like a piranha than a real estate agent. Brennan thought she would have covered the dead woman's body with a lampshade if this had been an 'open house'.

'That's helpful, thanks. Do you want the guys to have a look at you? Looks like you've had a nasty fall.'

'No, it's just a scratch,' Ambah said, as she touched her cheek gently with her fingers.

'I need to get your details. You'll have to come down to the station so we can get a full statement. Here's my card. I also have to ask you if you've touched anything?'

'No, of course not,' Ambah replied, offended by the police officer's insinuation.

'Can I also ask you again Ambah, to step outside?'

'Okay.' Ambah was ready to leave anyway. She had seen everything she needed to see.

French escorted Ambah to the front door and made sure she left this time. When he walked back down the hall he called to his partner, 'Hey Jill, what'll we do with the cat?' He poked his head around the corner of the kitchen with the cat cradled in his arms.

Jill smiled at her lanky off-sider. She liked Daniel French, he was easy going and dependable. Just the sort of traits she valued in a partner. 'Have a look in the cupboards, see if you can find something for the cat to eat, then ring the RSPCA and explain the situation. The family can decide what they want to do with it.'

Jill returned her attention to Cooke who was standing next to the woman's body. She smiled at him. 'Good idea not to disturb anything.'

'We'll be careful, don't worry.'

Rimis walked through the front door and down the hall into the kitchen. The first thing he noticed when he entered, apart from the smell of Rose's decomposing body, was the empty bottle of Scotch on the draining-board next to the kitchen sink. 'Looks like the old lady enjoyed a drink.'

Jill Brennan didn't hear him enter the room. She looked up from her notebook, startled.

'*Highland Park* – an expensive drop for someone who looks like they were down on their luck.' Rimis flashed Brennan his ID. 'We'll need to call in the Crime Scene Police. Give them a call will you?'

Jill realised that Nick Rimis wasn't interested in pleasantries as he picked up the empty whisky bottle from the drainer and looked at the label.

'There's one thing I do know, Brennan, and that's an expensive bottle of Scotch when I see one.'

Brennan looked over her shoulder at the bottle on the sink and made the call.

'Looks like she topped herself. Have a look around for a note and check her bedroom. You might also want to check who her doctor was and find out what meds she was on. Then you and French can go and notify the next of kin.'

Brennan gathered up the bottle and the empty packet of tablets and placed them in a large plastic zip lock bag and marked the label with the time, date and location.

'What's this?' Rimis bent over and picked up the corner of the business card from under the table with the tips of his fingers. 'Ambah St John. Residential Sales Consultant.'

'The real estate agent must have dropped it when she was snooping around.' Jill Brennan rolled her eyes. Rimis handed her the card and she put it inside the file beside the one Ambah had already given her.

Ambah St John was standing on the nature strip looking back at the house when Kevin Taggart walked up to her. He stood quietly beside her for a moment before he offered his outstretched hand and introduced himself. As if on cue, a bank of clouds, thick with moisture drifted in from the south and a flash of lightning raced across the sky in the distance. A heavy raindrop landed on Kevin Taggart's nose. He wiped it away, turned and looked at Ambah. She was staring back at the house, deep in thought.

'She probably died from pneumonia,' Kevin announced. He was waiting for her to agree with his theory or at least to make a comment. 'There are charities and community groups who look after people in trouble. Pride, particularly when you're old, is a dangerous trait. Don't you think?' He realised she'd not been listening to a word he said, he had seen that look before on other women's faces. She brushed past him and walked towards her car.

Ambah wasn't interested in what Kevin Taggart had to say, she thought he was a creep. She had been looking at the house and mentally going through a list of prospective buyers. At the moment she was only interested in the commission she would receive from the sale and knew she wouldn't have any trouble selling the house; she already had someone in mind and knew deceased estates sold quickly. Potential buyers always thought they were getting a bargain and 15 Eden Street would be no exception. The fact that Rose Phillips had died in the kitchen wouldn't make any difference, she thought, or would it?

Ambah hobbled over to her parked car. The heel of one of her shoes had snapped when she slipped on the front steps as she was leaving the house and her awkward gait reminded Kevin of Charlie Chaplin. All she needed was a walking stick to complete the picture in his mind. He watched as she slipped behind the steering wheel of her black Audi and threw him a backhanded wave. Ambah knew all the rules of selling real estate and one of them was that it didn't pay to get off side with the neighbours, no matter what you thought of them. She pushed her sunglasses back onto her head and put the car into drive. Even though she had been shaken by the morning's discovery, the thought of a large commission soothed her nerves. After all, no big deal, the woman was old, and everyone has to die sometime.

'Pride goeth before a fall and a haughty spirit before destruction,' Kevin called after Ambah as she drove up Eden Street and turned left into Parklands.

Chapter Five

'Excuse me, William, the police are here to see you,' Anita led the two officers into his office and closed the door behind her on her way out.

If William Phillips was surprised, he didn't show it. He stood and pushed his chair back from his desk. They were both fresh-faced kids and looked as if they had just graduated from the Academy. William imagined that they would be more at home by a roadside in the middle of the night attending a crash scene, than standing here in his plush office with the antique carpets on the floor and expensive art work on the walls. He noticed the female officer looking at the Joan Miró painting hanging on the wall behind him. She was obviously drawing her own conclusions as to the type of person he was.

William sized them up quickly, the way he usually did when he met a client for the first time. She was short, solidly built, but had a pleasing body, even though it was concealed behind an ill-fitting uniform. Her straight mousey-blonde hair was neatly tied back in a no-nonsense ponytail, making her look even younger than she probably was. He couldn't help but notice the Glock in her holster sitting neatly on her hip. Her sidekick was spotty faced and tall, and William wondered how he would hack it in a tight situation. They flashed their IDs at him and introduced themselves.

'Senior Constable Jill Brennan.'

'Constable Daniel French.' They nodded, straight-faced as they each shook William's hand. They were fidgeting with their caps, looking at each other, half expecting the other would take the initiative and speak first. Finally, it was Brennan who broke the silence by addressing William in a clear and in an almost too confident voice. 'Side kick' looked down at his polished boots concentrating too hard William thought, perhaps he was hoping to see his reflection in them.

'Mr Phillips, we need to ask you a few questions,' Brennan said.

As the female police officer looked down at her notes William wondered what was coming next. He was sure he had paid all his outstanding speeding fines and was puzzled by their unexpected presence in his office.

'Can you tell us your mother's full name and address, please?'

William worked the back of his neck with his fingers, looked into her eyes which were framed by thick lashes and answered her question. 'What's all this about anyway, officer?'

Brennan cleared her throat. 'Unfortunately, I have some sad news, Mr Phillips. It's your mother.

She was found dead this morning in her home. A real estate agent found her in the kitchen.'

William's head began to spin; he grabbed the side of his desk and sank slowly into his chair before inviting them to take a seat. 'What happened?' he asked.

'We're not sure at this stage. We don't know the circumstances surrounding her death.'

William and Brennan locked eyes. He was searching for answers and wondered if she knew more than she was letting on.

'Mr Phillips, can I ask how old your mother was?' She was holding a police issue note pad and William wondered how many times she had delivered news like this.

A knock on the paneled door broke the silence. Anita slipped into the office and set down a cup of milky tea in front of William. 'Can I offer you anything officers? Would you like tea, coffee?'

'Nothing, thank you.' Brennan replied for both of them.

William sipped from the white china teacup. The tea was hot and sweet and it coated the back of his throat as he swallowed. He thought of his mother and took another sip. The cup chinked against the saucer as he set it down. As he turned his thoughts back to his mother, he concentrated on how old she was as he massaged the back of his neck again, a quirky habit he had when he was exhausted, troubled by work or by something he was feeling deep inside and didn't want to talk about. He replied that she was eighty-five, not eighty-six until her birthday at the end of the year, which he realised after he had said it, was a dumb thing to say.

'I'm afraid you'll have to identify your mother's body. Do you think you'll be capable of doing that or can you suggest someone else who could do it on your behalf?' Brennan asked.

Anita slipped out of the office quietly closing the door behind her and William realised the whole office would soon know about his mother.

'Mr Phillips?' Brennan was waiting for an answer to her question.

William knew there *was* nobody else. 'No, I'll do it.' His voice was hoarse and his face paled beneath his suntan. He coughed to clear his throat.

'Mr Phillips, I'm not sure if you realise, but because your mother hasn't seen a GP in the last three months, by law, an autopsy needs to be performed to determine the cause of her death.' Brennan wondered if William Phillips had heard a single word of what she had just said.

He nodded, his face crumpled.

'If you have any questions, or if we can be of any further assistance, don't hesitate to give us a call.' Jill was standing over him now and impulsively she placed her hand gently on his shoulder. He looked up at her, surprised. She stepped away embarrassed. She and French handed their cards to him. He took them and placed them on his desk.

'Is there anyone we can call to be with you?' French asked kindly.

'No, there's nobody.'

'You sure?' Brennan asked.

'Yes, really. I just need some time for all of this to sink in.'

As the two officers left his office, William remained motionless at his desk. The reception area outside his door was deserted and the noisy background buzz of what was usually a busy office, was surprisingly quiet. He looked at the ivory coloured business cards sitting in front of him, examined the solid wording, then tucked Senior Constable Brennan's card in the top pocket of his business shirt and threw Constable French's in the waste paper bin.

William stood and walked towards the bank of windows which looked out across Sydney Harbour. The dark clouds which had been hovering around earlier in the morning had all but disappeared and the sun was now shining. He rested his closed fists on his narrow waist and with his flat, glassy eyes looking back at him, he saw the pride and stubbornness in them, the result of a working life spent asserting the rights of others. He still had a youthful look about him for a fifty-four year old and as he combed his fingers through his hair, a loose strand fell across his eyes and he realised he needed a haircut.

William Phillips had put in the hard yards, worked long hours, made all the important deadlines and had delivered 'the goods'. The sacrifices he'd made in his personal life had paid off. He was a corporate counsel in Lewis Stockland, a leading city merchant bank and he wasn't ashamed of the means by which he had used his contacts and colleagues to get to where he was. Considering his humble beginnings, sitting in a swanky corner office on the fifty-second floor of a prestigious office building located in the heart of Sydney's financial district was something of which he was proud.

Now as he looked out at the breathtaking harbour view, his thoughts turned to his wife and hoped Suellyn didn't have anything to do with the death of his mother. It was all he could think of when he dialed their home phone number. It was engaged. 'Typical,' he thought. He hung up. He would try again later. He was still clutching the handset, staring at the whites of his knuckles, contemplating what he would do next, when he wondered how long his mother had been dead before her body had been discovered. The police said a real estate agent had found her in the kitchen. That didn't make any sense to him, no sense at all. What was his mother doing making appointments with real estate agents? She didn't even own the Eden Street house, technically Suellyn did. It had been bought in her name for tax reasons. William knew that Suellyn had been trying to persuade his mother to move to a retirement village for months. He'd told his wife to leave her alone, told her she was wasting her time. He knew his mother and knew she was stubborn enough not to allow herself to be happy living anywhere else. He wasn't surprised when Suellyn told him Rose had said that the only way she was leaving the house was in a pine box. Rose Phillips was one hell of a stubborn woman and she wasn't going to be told what to do by her daughter-in-law or by anyone else for that matter.

The last time William had spoken to his mother was in a café in the city almost ten years ago. They had both said things to each other, things that perhaps shouldn't have been said, and now, it was too late. He had told her that he couldn't forgive her deceit, no matter what the reason and he regretted that now, regretted that he didn't give her the chance to explain and that she had been too proud and too stubborn not to make him listen. In hindsight, she was his mother and that should have counted for something. But Rose Phillips never attempted to contact her son, and they never spoke to each other again. William realised it was now too late for apologies, too late for anything. Death was permanent.

William walked out of his office an hour after the police had left. He'd been working on the Bellamy case before the police arrived and as he gathered the loose papers on his desk, he suddenly felt older than he was supposed to feel. He shoved the file and his phone into his leather briefcase and didn't say a word to anyone as he locked the door to his office and walked down the corridor towards the lifts. The call button lit up. Anita was sitting at her work station with her back to him and he was glad that she had the good sense not to speak to him. Anita Lewis knew William Phillips and knew his moods. His head was throbbing and he hoped that when the lift door eventually opened, it would be empty. He wasn't in any frame of mind to speak to anyone. A high pitched ding announced the lift's arrival. It startled him at first, but when he realised it was on the way down, he sighed with relief. He stepped into the lift and stared past his black Florsheims to the swirling dusty-green circles in the carpet, anything to take his mind off his mother.

'Sorry to hear the bad news, Mr Phillips.'

William turned his head towards the voice. Gavin McLeod, a first year graduate, looked at him from the corner of the lift with heavy-lidded eyes and acne pocked skin. He was holding an armful of documents against his chest and was on his way down to the twenty-eighth floor. It was lunchtime and William thought as he looked at him, that there was probably a soggy homemade sandwich in a paper bag waiting for him back at his desk. 'What was that Gavin?'

'Your mother, Mr Phillips.' Gavin was suddenly embarrassed, his face turned crimson and relief washed over him as the lift door suddenly opened at the twenty-eighth floor and he stepped out into the carpeted hall.

'Thanks,' was the only word William Phillips had thought to say to him.

When the lift door opened at the ground floor, William walked briskly across the terrazzo-tiled foyer, conscious of the click-clacking of his leather soled shoes as he made his way towards the entrance of the building. The rotating glass doors spun him out onto the footpath. Jostled by the busy rush of the lunchtime crowd, he looked around in an emotional daze at the busyness of the city. Dark suited men and women with phones pressed hard against their ears, young female office workers in short skirts and high heels, carrying shopping bags, giggling, calling out to each other, a group of tourists holding city maps upside down.

'I'll go to the morgue later,' he thought to himself. Identifying his mother's body wasn't something he was looking forward to. He dodged a FedEx delivery van as he crossed Elizabeth Street against the traffic lights and headed towards the Botanical Gardens. The Gardens were usually packed at this time of day with crowds of office workers vying for the pick of the timber seats under the fig trees or else working up a sweat as they took to the bitumen paths and jogged around the Gardens' perimeter. A red, miniature tourist train packed with elderly tourists and parents with young children passed in front of him as he crossed the narrow path towards a grassy knoll near the Oriental Gardens. He found a semi-secluded spot under the canopy of a large Port Jackson fig and stood for a moment surveying the scene in front of him before he sat down on the cool grass and loosened the knot of his tie. He removed his jacket, folded it and placed it down beside him. With his legs sprawled out in front of him and his elbows supporting his weight, he gazed out across at the harbour and focused his attention on a container ship heading towards The Heads.

The Gardens were William's favourite place, especially at a time like this, at a time when he needed to think.

Chapter Six

Jill Brennan's business card sat in the middle of William Phillips's desk. He dialed her direct line and was surprised when a gravelly male voice answered. 'Could I speak with Senior Constable Brennan?'

William didn't have to wait long before her voice came onto the line.

'Brennan speaking.'

'Hello Senior Constable, this is William Phillips. You were in my office earlier today. I'm phoning about my mother, Rose Phillips.'

'Yes, of course. How can I help Mr Phillips?'

'I've just come from the morgue. The autopsy is scheduled for Monday and I'm keen to know when the results will be available. I know I should have asked them the details when I was there, maybe they even told me, but to be honest, I'm not really thinking very clearly at the moment.'

'The Coroner usually takes about two or three days to make a determination. I'll let you know the results when we receive the report, and Mr Phillips, I want to offer my personal condolences. I know it must have been a terrible shock for you this morning. You may want to contact the counselling service, they'll be able to give you any information you might need. I've got their phone number here somewhere. If you want to hold on, I'll get it for you.' She flicked through the files on her desk and found the number she was looking for. When she was shown into William Phillips's office earlier that day, Jill Brennan had been overwhelmed by his good looks and the plush office environment in which she had found herself. When she spotted the Miró original hanging on the wall behind his desk, she was blown away. Brennan had enough art books to stock a small library in the small flat she rented in a trendy part of the city, everything from Cezanne to Picasso.

The young Senior Constable was an intelligent thirty year old and her wide, infectious smile matched her outgoing personality. She toyed with the idea of becoming an art curator after she finished a Master's Degree, majoring in Art History, at Sydney University, but spent two years working and travelling in Europe instead until she returned to Sydney, jobless. Disillusioned with the art world and looking for a complete change, a friend suggested the armed forces. She chose the police force instead because she was naive enough to think she could make a difference. At the top of her graduating year at the academy, her superiors were quick to notice her abilities and now after five years of general policing, she was ready to make a move into Criminal Investigations now that she had completed her training.

William looked at the leather pen holder on his

desk and picked out a black pen. 'Thanks for the number, I'll give them a call.' He scribbled the sequence of numbers on the back of her card and tried not to sound like a victim. William wasn't a criminal barrister and was way out of his comfort zone on this one. He'd been doodling absentmindedly on his writing pad, a messy habit he had when he was up against a difficult problem and had to find a solution, and quickly. He replaced the phone in its cradle and threw Jill Brennan's card into the top drawer of his desk. The writing pad he had been scribbling on was stained with coffee mug rings and ink-smudged scribble. 'Jill' in light flowery letters stood out from the page. He lent back and balanced on his office chair with his hands behind his head. It was time to go home. It was a waste of time sitting at his desk expecting to do some work. The Bellamy case would have to wait.

William drove his black *S* Class Mercedes into the basement of the Panorama Apartments and parked next to Suellyn's Porsche in the second of the car spaces marked sixteen. The fluorescent lighting in the garage bounced off the concrete walls and before opening the driver's door he reached into the backseat and grabbed his jacket and briefcase. The high pitched blip of the car alarm echoed through the car park and he noticed a small, white van which belonged to the building superintendent, parked near the entrance as he walked towards the lifts.

It was late afternoon but early enough that most people were still at work. It was unusual for him to be home at this hour and as he checked his Rolex he wondered if Suellyn had gone for a walk as she usually did at this time of day or if she was at home now, pouring over some women's magazine, thinking about what she would prepare for dinner or what restaurant they would eat out at if she was too tired to cook. William wasn't looking forward to telling Suellyn about his mother. He knew she was emotionally unstable when he married her, 'flighty' was the word his friends had used to describe her, but she had her good points, though he couldn't quite remember what they were now after twelve years of marriage. He usually tried to avoid situations that would have her flying into a fit of hysterics, but he didn't have a choice now, he would have to tell her before she found out from someone else. The lift was taking its time and as he stood with his back against the wall with his hands in his pockets, he realised it wasn't the first time that day, that he had wondered how his mother had died. He still couldn't believe it. His body began to shake, his palms were hot and sweaty, beads of perspiration formed on his upper lip. Delayed shock, he guessed. It wasn't surprising, it *had* been a shock, one hell of a shock, the news of his mother's death was one thing, but having to identify her body, well that was something else altogether. Her decomposed body was concealed by a crisp white shroud and only her face was on show. He now understood why a dead person's pallor was often described as ghostly. His mother's face was ghostly all right, ghostly grey with a greenish tinge added for good measure, like powdery embers in a cold fireplace and with her saggy skin taking on the signs of decay, she had not been a pretty sight. The experience of observing a decomposed body had been one which he hoped he would never have to repeat.

William's thoughts turned to when he and his mother lived together at Dora Valentine's boarding house, the days before Eden Street. His mother was an attractive, outgoing type of woman then, full of fun and brimming with life. She was the type of woman who never asked for help but was always there, ready to help others.

She had always been in good health, at least she was the last time he saw her. But that was ten years ago. A lot can happen in a person's life in ten years and Rose probably wouldn't have told him if there was a problem with her health or if she had any other issues for that matter. Rose walked everywhere out of necessity because she had never learned to drive. With a bus at the front door and a train station a few blocks away, there had never been any need when she lived at Dora's boarding house in the city. He knew from Suellyn that she walked to the shopping centre at least once a week to buy groceries, so he had assumed she must have been in reasonably good health.

William regretted that he'd not gone to see her and resolve the business regarding his father. He cleared his throat and wiped his eyes as he realised it was too late now for any explanations from his mother or forgiveness on his part. Pride and stubbornness had got in the way, as it always did in people's lives. He wondered what she did to fill her days, wondered what her life had become without him. The glass paneled lift door opened abruptly onto the eighth floor. He inserted the key in the lock until it turned and clicked. *Jumping Jack Flash* from one of Suellyn's Rolling Stones albums was pumping loudly and he realised, not for the first time, that Suellyn's taste in music was quite different from his own.

The sliding doors to the terrace were wide open and a chilly but gentle sea breeze whistled around the apartment. The smell of coffee brewing tainted the air and the ocean shimmered like cut glass. A mob of surfers in wet suits bobbed up and down on their boards, waiting for the next set. They floated like champagne corks as they drifted towards the shore and William knew he would be joining them after he broke the news of Rose's death to Suellyn.

'Suellyn,' he called out above the loud music.

His wife walked out of the kitchen dressed in a pair of navy designer jeans and a white linen blouse tied up in a knot. Her honey coloured midriff was showing and her feet were cloaked in thick blue socks. A look of surprise swept across her face when she saw William standing in the lounge-room. Before he had a chance to say anything, she took a bite from the thick wholemeal sandwich she was holding in her hand. The sight of Dijon mustard on her cheek would have made him laugh under normal circumstances.

'What are you doing home so early? Someone die?' she asked with a full mouth.

William collapsed onto the white leather lounge. He struggled with his tie for a moment then decided to remove his shoes instead. He threw his feet up on the leather ottoman with his black cotton socked feet spread out in front of him. 'Get us both a drink will you,' he said, 'and turn that music off.'

Suellyn put her sandwich down on the glass coffee table sensing that William had something important to tell her. She saw the tension etched across his face. He looked exhausted and she thought, not for the first time, that he was beginning to look his age. Suellyn poured them both a strong whisky and dropped in a few ice cubes from the bar fridge. She handed him a tumbler of the golden liquid and waited for him to speak.

'It's Rose,' he paused then gulped down the Scotch until only a mouthful remained. 'She's dead.'

Suellyn looked at him. A perfect 'O' suddenly formed on her lips. 'Oh my God. What happened?' She put the tumbler down on the coffee table next to her half-eaten sandwich and stared at William waiting for him to speak again.

'They don't know, she's at the Glebe Morgue. I had to go and identify her body. She's been dead for at least three days. Suellyn, she died all alone.' Suellyn placed her hand over her mouth and for once, couldn't think of anything to say.

'The autopsy is scheduled for first thing Monday morning.' William's voice faltered.

Suellyn swirled her whisky around in her glass with her finger and looked at William. His body slumped and disappeared into itself as he sat motionless, his head in his hands, elbows on his thighs. 'You didn't have anything to do with it did you, William?'

William looked up at Suellyn, surprised and confused by her accusation. He rubbed his eyes with his fists.

'I was going to ask you the same question.'

Chapter Seven

Kevin Taggart lived in a brick bungalow between his two neighbours, Ashleigh Taylor who led a busy life and Rose Phillips who led no life at all. A redundancy package offered by his employer had seduced the former insurance assessor into accepting an early retirement which allowed him to devote what was to be the remainder of his life to his passion, landscape painting. He painted watercolors mostly, because he liked the soft hews of peaceful landscapes - mountains, seashores and small boats lying on their sides, cast adrift on remote beaches somewhere in his imagination. He thought of himself as a talented artist even though he had never had an exhibition. When he didn't win a prize at the local community art show earlier in the year, he was disappointed; disappointed that he'd not at least received a highly commended award. However, he was convinced that it was only a matter of time, before someone, somewhere, would recognise his talent.

When Ashleigh Taylor moved into the neighbourhood, he was second in line behind the Blake sisters to introduce himself and welcome her to Eden Street. Kevin wasn't sure what she did for a living, but he knew she worked long hours. When she left the house at odd hours of the night, he would listen to the moan of the garage door and the roar of the diesel engine of her Landcruiser as it turned over and reversed up the driveway. He waited for her to return. Sometimes it wasn't until the early hours of the following morning when the sound of the roller door drifted across the side fence into his open bedroom window. Kevin didn't mind the disruption, he didn't sleep much anyway, he thought sleep was a waste of time, especially when he had so much on his mind and so much he had to achieve.

He had looked at her with an artist's eye. Ashleigh was not beautiful in the true sense of the word, but she was well proportioned, had an open face, long limbs and a trim, toned body. She had the milky white complexion of someone who spent too much time indoors. Her thick, wavy hair framed her face and was the colour of chestnuts. He liked the way she tucked it behind her ears, and the way it bobbed against her shoulders when she walked. But what struck Kevin mostly about Ashleigh Taylor, were her steely blue eyes. When he first looked into them, he recognised that they were the eyes of someone who had seen too much or had seen things, most people would not want to admit to seeing. With her expensive and conservative clothes and her confident manner, Kevin was puzzled by the fact that she was living alone in a modest house next to his. He wondered if she was a sex worker.

Kevin had an excellent memory. He was not a religious man although he recited biblical verses to himself as he painted, when his mind was lucid and his body relaxed. He made a point when visiting the Blake sisters, to recite a verse to them and they appeared to enjoy his 'pearls of wisdom' as they called them. He had warned the Blake sisters and Rose Phillips many times, that their stubbornness and pride would lead to trouble one day.

Kevin felt a strong sense of responsibility towards his elderly neighbours. He felt sorry for them, especially as they led such lonely and insignificant lives. With no family to speak of, he felt it was his duty to keep a watchful eye on them; he wanted to make sure they were coping with their lives and did his best to make them comfortable, just as he had done with Nora, his elderly mother.

Kevin Taggart had not known his father, he was absent from his life from its very beginning. His mother was a proud woman who strongly believed in the will of God. A religious woman, her flat, cold, eyes looked out onto the world with a great deal of displeasure. She wore a perpetual scowl on her face. Hers was a life filled with disappointments, the biggest disappointment being her son, Kevin, and she had never missed an opportunity to tell him so.

A personality disorder was suggested in hushed tones to Kevin by well-meaning people who tried to help him deal with his difficult mother. Kevin was with her, when in her eighty-first year, she suddenly died. He hoped for her sake that if there was such a place as the next life, that it would be a great deal more satisfactory to her than the one she had lived with him in Eden Street.

Kevin's studio, attached to the back of his house, was built when he realised he needed extra space after his bedroom and lounge-room disappeared beneath the clutter of his life. He spent most of his waking hours there and when he closed the door behind him, he tuned into his favourite classical radio station and turned the volume up loud.

Rose Phillips didn't say anything of course about the studio when it was built without Council approval. She wasn't the type of woman to complain about anything. The studio, unlike the rest of his house, was uncluttered and organised. A scrubbed oak table was pushed up against a wall and on it stood a large, empty, juice tin filled with cheap brushes. The assortment consisted of brushes of different sizes and thicknesses. Pencils and crayons were also on the table and were neatly placed, side-by-side, sorted by colour and size. A cheap timber A-framed easel stood in the middle of the room and a shaft of light streamed through a permanently opened window. The floor was covered with timber patterned linoleum; it was cheap, serviceable and easy to clean. The windows were bare; Kevin didn't see the need for curtains.

Kevin Taggart found comfort and pleasure in his painting. It stilled his mind. He began attending art classes after his mother died because of the depression which had descended upon him after her departure from his life. He realised he needed something apart from prescription drugs to calm his shattered nerves. The walls of Kevin's house were covered with his paintings. His artistic style had changed recently from landscape painting and he was excited about the direction in which his creativity was taking him. He was experimenting, looking for ways he could bring more depth to his work. One of his completed works sat proudly on the easel in the middle of the studio. Satisfied with the result, he stood back from it now, admiring it from different angles according to the light. It was different from his usual landscapes, it was dark and menacing. Distorted faces of crone-like women emerged from behind grotesque figures, and unidentifiable shapes sprung from the dark shadows. Tufts of cat hair glued to the canvas were painted over with oxblood paint. A large red cross dominated the foreground.

Kevin's studio was oriented towards Ashleigh Taylor's backyard and from his window the side gate to her house was in full view. The back door slammed. Ashleigh was dressed in a black tracksuit with white stripes running down the side of the legs and runners which were too white not to be brand new. She wore a bright yellow ribbon which held her hair off her neck. Kevin squeezed two blobs of red paint onto his palette and as he mixed the paint, his mind began to wander. He imagined that Ashleigh must observe a lot on her walks, people coming and going, small children being called inside by their mothers after playing, people going about their daily lives, middle aged women hoping to shed weight delivering shopping catalogues, tradesmen fixing things, watching, silently observing. Similar to what he enjoyed doing. He liked to observe people, to feel as if he was part of their lives.

He was aware of Ashleigh's movements and knew that she walked every day, but not always at the same time. He spied her at the shops, often at the patisserie in the arcade next to the news agency and wondered what type of pastries she liked. Perhaps he would surprise her one day and invite her in for afternoon tea.

Kevin's thoughts turned to Rose Phillips. He knew that she had been someone who had a lot on her mind and far too much spare time to think. He had known of her pain and he wanted to help her deal with it. On occasions he spoke to her across the side fence hoping to bring some happiness to her life. He knew elderly people enjoyed a cup of tea and a friendly chat and he had invited her in for tea on more than one occasion, but she had declined his offers. There had been a falling out between Rose and her son, over some family matter. He never asked her the details, it was none of his business. Her daughter-in-law visited occasionally, he knew because he recognised her car, a shiny black Porsche. She looked a tough nut that one, Kevin thought. He'd met that sort before, done up to the nines in smart clothes with a slick hairdo. Thought the world owed her something.

Kevin saw much of what went on in Eden Street. He visited the Blake sisters regularly and enjoyed friendly conversations and cheap sherry which they served in crystal glasses. He carried out small handyman jobs for them. Last winter, he nailed their front window shut because Edi had complained of a draught. Kevin thought it was a good thing when you helped your neighbours and he knew that if you helped them often enough, something good would come from it. Edi and Rhoda bought one of Kevin's watercolours to hang on their lounge-room wall. They were impressed by the painting and made a fuss of him when he showed it to them. They told him they thought he was talented and Kevin had been deeply flattered by their words of encouragement. The painting reminded them of when they were girls growing up on the far North Coast. They offered to pay him and at first he said it wasn't necessary, it was meant as a gift, but when Rhoda went to her black purse she kept in the top drawer of the dresser and pulled out five, crisp, one hundred dollar notes, what could he say? Not wishing to offend them, he gratefully accepted the money and went straight out and bought a supply of paint and two sable paint brushes.

Chapter Eight

It was Saturday morning, the autumn air was crisp and clean. Ashleigh Taylor licked the tips of her fingers before flicking through the travel and leisure section of the weekend newspaper. She was mildly interested in an article on wine and cycling tours of Tuscany but didn't read past the first paragraph. Her life was too busy to even consider a holiday. Her work load was horrendous and staff shortages were a fact of life. A cafetière of coffee sat on the outdoor table in front of her and after she emptied her third cup, she decided against pouring herself another and folded the newspaper in half and put it to one side. The morning air filled her lungs and her face began to soften, her body relaxed as she took in a deep breath.

Ashleigh preferred the cooler months of autumn and winter to the sticky, claustrophobic heat of summer. She welcomed the promise of frosty mornings and blue Wedgewood skies, of cosy winter evenings at home devouring crumpets, licking up the sticky, buttery droplets of honey as they dribbled down the sides of her hands. Ashleigh ran her fingers through her thick, unruly locks and massaged her scalp. Her eyes were red-rimmed and puffy. It had been a late night last night; a drunken brawl outside a city hotel had resulted in a teenager's death. She covered her mouth with her hand to suppress a yawn then reached down and pulled off her sheepskin boots. She padded down the timber steps into the backyard. The wet grass caressed the soles of her feet as she dug her toes into the lawn.

The backyard and the garden beds were overgrown. Pruning and a dose of 'blood and bone' could be the answer, even though she knew nothing at all about gardening. Another job to add to her list of things to do and she made a mental note to google 'garden landscaping contractors' when she went back inside. Order needed to be brought back into the rambling yard and if there was anything Ashleigh Taylor craved, it was order. Without it, her life was a mess. An unruly row of unidentifiable bushes pushed up against the neighbour's fence. She imagined that they had once been part of a neatly, trimmed hedge, the result of a keen gardener's eye for detail. Now, it was nothing more than a sprawling, shapeless mass. It had been neglected for too long; holes yawned giving the hedge a vulnerable and hapless appearance.

A lemon tree with a gnarled trunk stood a few metres away from where she was standing. With the palms of her hands resting on her hips, Ashleigh studied the tree, wondering if its strength and vigor lay in its neglect. People, like gardens, needed to be tended and nurtured, some more than others. Buttery-coloured lemons lay at her feet and as she bent over and gathered them up she pulled at the bottom edge of her jumper, stretching it out as far as it would go before placing the lemons into the woollen pouch. The fruits were bruised and the heat from her body aroused a heady aroma of lemon oil, reawakening memories of winter afternoons in her mother's garden and the sickly sweet taste of homemade lemonade.

The low grumble of a lawn mower starting up caused her to forget the lemons for a moment and she looked across at her neighbour's backyard. Kevin Taggart was standing by his rusty tin shed. The mower came to an abrupt stop. With his body bent and his back towards her, Ashleigh watched her neighbour as he began to clean the mower with a dirty rag. The T-shirt he was wearing had a large rip under the left armpit and his faded, navy track suit pants were splattered with flecks of white and yellow paint, reminding her of an artist's palette. His back was weak and flabby and as he leaned backwards on his haunches, she caught sight of a small bald patch on the crown of his head. Thin wispy strands of dull, grey hair lay flat against the shiny patch which was smooth and moist from his exertion. He must have sensed her watching him because he turned and gave her an easy smile.

'Damn mower, she starts then conks out. Probably a bit of dirt in the carburetor.'

Ashleigh wasn't sure how to respond. She didn't know anything about lawnmowers. When she thought about it, she had never even owned one, never mind trying to start one. To break the awkward silence between them, Ashleigh grabbed a lemon from her jumper. She felt a little foolish now, standing there in front of him with her outstretched jumper spilling over with lemons. 'Would you like some Kevin? There are too many here for me.' Ashleigh looked down at her jumper straining from the weight of the thick-skinned fruit. She lowered it and wondered what she would do with them if he declined her offer. Perhaps she would make lemon butter. She was sure she had a recipe somewhere.

'Thanks, that's kind of you,' Kevin said. 'I like lemon in my tea.'

Ashleigh passed half of the lemons over the fence and dropped the remainder on the ground in front of her. He looked at her uncomfortably as if he had something important he needed to say. As they stood together enjoying the warmth of the early morning sunshine and the banter of light hearted conversation, Kevin suddenly stopped in mid-sentence and turned the conversation around to the tragic death of their neighbour. They had been in the middle of discussing who made the best coffee in the village when he asked had she known that their neighbour was found dead in her kitchen yesterday morning. He went on to tell her that a young real estate agent had found her body and how she had gone out of her way to introduce herself to him when they met on the footpath outside Rose's house. She had described to him in detail, the miserable circumstances in which their neighbour had been living and the appalling way in which she had died.

Ashleigh was surprised to learn of Rose's death and as Kevin delivered a detailed description of her decomposed body, she wondered what his relationship to the elderly recluse had been. He followed on with a description of the inside of the house, telling her how it smelt of cat piss, and large patches of flaking paint were peeling from the ceilings and walls, a missing glass window pane had been replaced with a clump of brown, waxy wrapping paper and sticky tape. Ashleigh looked past him and across to Rose's backyard.

'I can't imagine what life was like for her, can you Kevin? What a terrible way to live and a lonely way to die.' Ashleigh's lips parted slightly; she realised she was speaking more to herself than to Kevin.

During her work when she was a key player in the tragedies of other people's lives, Ashleigh Taylor knew that it was almost impossible to control the circumstances under which a person lived or died. A person's life could easily become stuck, like a stylus on a record player trapped in a groove on a vinyl record, playing over and over and over again, spinning around with no means of escape. At least not until someone or something stopped the music. Ashleigh wondered if life had simply become too much for Rose Phillips.

As Kevin and Ashleigh stood by the dividing fence a black crow squawked and swooped down in front of them. The crow looked at them with glassy-yellow eyes and raised its head before it flew off to the north. Kevin didn't look up as Ashleigh had done to see what had caused the bird to take flight, he was looking down at the ground, concentrating on his scuffed, paint stained joggers. Without warning, he jerked his head upwards, just as the crow had done, his troubled eyes met Ashleigh's and he looked at her as if he had just remembered something which he felt he should share with her. He didn't speak, but she saw the expression on his face and the bright tears which had sprung up in his eyes. A solitary tear fell softly and quickly became trapped in one of the deep crevasses of his face. He wiped the tear away roughly with his thumb and whispered in a soft, almost inaudible voice.

'Pride goeth before a fall and a haughty spirit before destruction.'

'What was that you said Kevin?' Ashleigh asked, not too unkindly.

Kevin coughed and cleared his throat, embarrassed by his sudden outburst. 'Perhaps I should have done more for Mrs Phillips,' he said. 'But she was such a proud, stubborn woman, she never asked anyone for help, not even me, someone I always hoped she would come to consider as a friend.'

'How were you to know if she needed help Kevin? She was obviously a very private person. When does anyone know when to intrude into someone's life? There's a fine line between caring and interfering Kevin, everyone knows that.' Having said that, the saddest thing, Ashleigh realised was that Rose Phillips didn't appear to have anybody in her life who really cared about her, even a little. Ashleigh said she must have been lonely living in the house by herself but Kevin replied that she did have a cat. They both wondered what had happened to it.

'Well, I think I'll go and make myself some lemon tea.' Kevin performed a juggling act with the lemons, threw them into the air, caught them one by one, placed them in the side pockets of his tracksuit pants and slowly backed away from the fence.

'Great juggling, Kevin,' Ashleigh said. She bent over to pick up the lemons at her feet and as she raised her head she said as an afterthought, 'enjoy your lemon tea.' But Kevin had already retreated inside. Despite his outburst and display of emotion, Ashleigh couldn't shake off the feeling that Kevin was insincere when they were discussing Rose's death. What was it anyway with those verses about pride and stubbornness? Ashleigh's curiosity was aroused and she began to wonder if Rose had been neglectful in paying her bills or if she was financially unable. Was this the reason the electricity had been disconnected? Were there wads of money stashed away in a rusty biscuit tin somewhere in the back of a kitchen cupboard, lost and long forgotten or was she too proud, as Kevin had suggested, and unable to ask for help?

Ashleigh sat down on the back steps of the verandah and realised it must have been Rose Phillips who had smiled at her only a few days before when she pulled into her driveway after a long night. She remembered her shy, curious smile, a smile from someone who was not used to smiling at strangers. She conjured up Rose's image in her mind, concentrating hard, she tried to recall every detail about her. The woman was petite. Her hair was grey and wiry and a few strands strayed from under the bright yellow, woollen beret she was wearing. The beret was perched high on the top of her head with two matching woollen pompoms dangling from the crown. They had looked ridiculous Ashleigh remembered thinking at the time. They stood out like beacons and were the only sign of colour in her drab appearance. They bounced and swayed in time to her small steps. Her stick like, stockinged legs poked out from beneath a thick coat which hung loosely from her shoulders and was splashed with flecks which looked like flakes of snow. The coat material had been popular once. Ashleigh regretted that she'd not acknowledged her, that she didn't push down the automatic window button and call out after her, a 'good morning'.

Doctor Ashleigh Taylor was a senior forensic pathologist with the New South Wales Coroner's office. From the beginning of her professional life she had been on a journey of discovery. Intelligent and astute, she had been trained in the art of observation and while searching for signs and clues left on the lifeless bodies laid out before her on the metallic examination tables, she felt responsible for every one of them and for the friends and families left behind who had loved them. Loved ones looking for answers, left confused by sudden, unexpected deaths, not knowing how to deal with their grief. It was more than a job to Ashleigh Taylor, for her it was about taking in the evidence, doing the work and knowing at the end of the day she would come up with the right answer.

Two days after Rose Phillips's body was discovered in her kitchen, a small red van packed with 'For Sale' and 'For Lease' signs pulled away from the curb in front of 15 Eden Street. Left behind and planted firmly in the front yard stood a large 'For Sale' sign with a photograph of the house and a large red 'Deceased Estate' sticker slammed across the face of it.

'Didn't take them long,' Ashleigh mumbled to herself as she peered into her letter box expecting to find a fistful of bills, but found instead two fat, slimy snails and a half eaten Pizza Hut brochure. She removed the snails and hurled them onto the road and tucked the Pizza Hut brochure into her pocket. She walked along the footpath and stopped in front of the 'For Sale' sign outside Rose's house. The Californian bungalow was in a terrible state. The ramshackle garden was overgrown, an outdated shade of green paint was peeling from the timber bargeboards and window casements and a number of terracotta tiles were missing from the roof. The house was below street level and Ashleigh imagined it would be cold in winter. A section of the brick fence, according to Kevin, had collapsed into the front yard and fallen onto the row of rose bushes with a whimper during the middle of the night years before. They managed to survive for a short time before they eventually withered and died. The bricks and the roses lay dormant now, buried and long forgotten.

Ashleigh crossed to the other side of the street and noticed not for the first time that a number of the houses, including her own, desperately needed renovation. The houses, neglected, unkempt and unloved, were much like the people who lived in them. Many of the elderly residents in Eden Street peered out through their thin, white polyester curtains, stubbornly holding on to their independence, worried that their well-meaning children would ship them off to a nursing home or retirement village at the first sign of forgetfulness or personal neglect.

Chapter Nine

Ashleigh discovered an envelope addressed 'to our new neighbour' on her front verandah. Inside was an invitation carefully written on cream coloured note paper from Edi and Rhoda Blake, inviting her to sherry and scones on Sunday afternoon, at three pm sharp.

A cool breeze slapped at Ashleigh's legs as she stood waiting on the marble doorstep. Three green tomatoes were neatly placed on the window sill, waiting for time or the sun's rays to ripen them. As a grandfather clock chimed the hour inside the house, Ashleigh caught sight of a grey, wrinkled face peering out from behind a lace curtain. A moment later the same face reappeared at the front door.

'Can I help you?' the woman asked politely in a quiet and gentle voice through a crack in the door. Her smell was faint and old-lady sweet.

'Hello, I'm Ashleigh Taylor. I'm your new neighbour from across the street. You invited me in for a drink.'

'Who is it, Edith?' came a shrill voice from the back of the house.

'It's the neighbour, she wants us to go out for a drink.'

Ashleigh smiled and wondered if she had made a mistake by coming.

'It's all right, Edi dear, it's our new neighbour. We invited her over, you remember don't you?' Rhoda moved her sister gently away from the door. 'Come in dear, I'm Rhoda and this is Edith. But you can call her Edi if you like. You must excuse her, she gets a little confused at times.'

Rhoda was a fine looking woman who looked as if she was approaching her eighties but could easily have passed for a woman ten years younger. Her hair was thick and grey; china blue eyes looked out from behind expensive glasses and around her neck she wore a pearl necklace. A set of matching earrings hung from her baggy lobes. She was dressed smartly in a mauve jumper and a check skirt and a pair of thick stockings covered her sturdy legs.

Edi on the other hand, looked frail and confused. A cardigan covered a crisp, white blouse and a pair of moccasins poked out from under her slacks. Her smart appearance did little to disguise her fish-like eyes which gave her a look that said to the world that she was unaware of who she was. Ashleigh wondered how long Edi would be able to live in the house before her sister could no longer take care of her.

Ashleigh attempted to make herself comfortable on the lumpy, red lounge. The gas heater was set on high, the room was stuffy and a little too warm for the time of day. The sun was beating through the front windows, which Ashleigh noticed were nailed shut. At her feet, a stain the size of a fifty-cent piece stared back at her from behind the faded pink swirls of carpet.

'Now, dear, I'll get you a sherry and we'll have a nice, long chat.' Rhoda moved towards the timber sideboard and poured the syrupy liquid from a crystal decanter into three glasses and placed them carefully on a tray. She offered Ashleigh a glass.

'Cheers,' Ashleigh said and smiled across at the two women.

'I suppose you have heard about our neighbour?' Rhoda asked as she put down her glass on the coffee table. 'Extremely tragic, such a pleasant woman you know.' Rhoda looked down at her lap and fiddled with her handkerchief, twisting the corners into little balls. 'Rose Phillips was a very private person. We invited her in for a sherry when she first arrived in Eden Street, didn't we Edi dear? That would have been a few years ago. I can't quite recall but it would have to be at least ten, don't you think Edi?' Edi was staring at the gas heater and made no attempt to reply. Rhoda paused and tried to remember. A look of irritation crossed her face as she attempted to recall the year but decided it wasn't an important fact in the telling of the story and continued. She looked at Ashleigh. 'I've lost track now. Of course, one does you know, when you get to our age.' Edi nodded in agreement.

The Blake sisters raised their glasses to their lips

in unison and sipped. Rhoda placed her glass down on the coffee table and paused for a moment. Ashleigh imagined she did this in order to gain her attention or it may have been that she was trying to recall a vital piece of information she felt she should share with her.

'Poor Rose, something awful must have happened between the two of them. I blame it all on the son. Rose became distant almost overnight. She just didn't want to know us and wasn't the same woman at all. Before all the business with her son, she would often drop in for a chat and a cup of tea on her way home from the shops and every Sunday morning she would walk with us to St Michael's to celebrate Mass. She was very involved in the Church activities, arranging the flowers, helping with the morning tea. But after the falling out, all that changed. I know she didn't like her daughter-in-law, she told us that much, but she was very proud of him you know. William was his name, but she always liked to call him Billy. She told us that he was a very important barrister and worked in a bank in the city.'

Rhoda gathered her thoughts and wiped her lips with a white linen serviette and continued. 'She died alone, right under our very noses. We were home last Friday; we could have helped had we known. You know dear - she was in her kitchen, drinking tea. Thank heavens for that real estate agent. It must have been quite a shock for such a young girl. Kevin told us all about it. He is very upset, the whole street is.' Rhoda wiped away a tear from the corner of her eye. 'We'll be going to the funeral of course. I suppose it will be sometime next week.'

Edi sat quietly, gazing out through the front window nursing her glass of sherry in her lap, watching for any movement in the street. A dog barked a lonely bark in the distance.

'Kevin said she died from pneumonia. Have you met Kevin?' Rhoda asked but didn't wait for Ashleigh's reply. 'Charming man, Kevin, and helpful too, always popping in to check on us, doing little odd jobs for no reward. He nailed our window shut last winter when we complained of a draught. He doesn't seem to have many visitors though, does he Edi?'

Rhoda offered another sherry and a jam covered scone which Edi had brought in on a plate from the kitchen. She wouldn't take no for an answer and as Rhoda refilled her glass, Ashleigh swallowed a mouthful of doughy scone and caught a whiff of her scent, a combination of sickly perfume and beeswax polish. The room was musty and damp. A nest of stackable timber tables, once popular in the sixties was pushed into a corner of the room. Crocheted doilies littered every flat surface like discarded sheets of notepaper. They looked as if they had been caught up by a sudden gust of wind and had landed there by luck, rather than by design. Landscapes by unknown artists hung from the picture rails together with prints of subdued English hunting scenes of muscled horses and their handsome red suited riders. A sequence of scenes at various stages of the hunt was strung out along the picture rails along the back wall of the room. Ashleigh moved into a more comfortable position on the lounge and shifted a cushion to one side.

Perhaps it was because Rhoda had finished talking

that Edi's face suddenly brightened. She appeared to emerge from a fog, smiled and asked politely, 'Now Ann, it's your turn. Tell us something about yourself.'

Rhoda winked at Ashleigh.

Ashleigh realised she had their full attention and as the sisters sat perched like cockatoos on their straight-backed chairs, they stared at her expectantly, waiting for her to speak. Ashleigh looked into their eager faces and wondered where she should begin.

Chapter Ten

It was Monday morning. Ashleigh hoped this week she would be able to catch up on some of the backlog of paper work sitting in her in tray. She walked at a leisurely pace along the corridor of the Glebe Mortuary, carrying a coffee in a polystyrene cup, ignoring her footsteps as they echoed on the polished linoleum floor. A bank of fluorescent lights lit the corridor and the cool light bounced off the bluish-green walls; she was headed for the autopsy suites. The double doors slid open as she keyed in the security code and walked into the white tiled room. She looked around for Sam. It was seven-fifteen; she was early. She knew the other pathologists and technicians wouldn't start arriving until at least eight-thirty.

The autopsy suite had two rows of seven metallic examination tables. The only difference between the room and a hospital operating theatre was that here, all the patients were dead. Ashleigh checked her phone for any messages before switching it off. She sat down at her desk and pulled out a muesli bar from her top drawer and unwrapped it. She was about to take a bite when Sam Lewis walked into her office.

'Mike's called in sick. Looks like you'll have to take his cases for today, Doc.'

Ashleigh returned the health bar to the drawer and stood up. 'Well let's get on with it then,' she sighed and looked at her in tray. It was going to be a long day.

Ashleigh followed Sam into the examination room. A pair of pale blue surgical gloves hung out from one of the pockets of her scrubs. She reached over and grabbed a glass jar from a row of specimen bottles lined up against the side wall. The contents of the jar offered little resistance as she dug her index finger into the solidified eucalyptus oil. The jelly like substance helped to mask the smells of the examination room, the disinfectant and the stench of decomposing bodies. This was something she had learnt from Doctor Ian Markham, her predecessor, who had introduced her to this trick of the trade on her first day on the job. The substance seared the inside of her nose. Sam Lewis suddenly appeared beside her. The morgue technician was holding a clipboard in his hands. He had been going through the day's list before Ashleigh had arrived and now he moved closer to her, close enough to feel her breath on him and smell her French perfume. 'No double dipping now, Doc,' he laughed as he inserted his finger into the jar and proceeded to prod the white substance up his left nostril. 'That should do the trick,' he said as he returned the jar to the shelf.

A gust of foul smelling, chilled air struck Ashleigh in the face when she opened the stainless steel refrigerator doors. The freezer held up to ten bodies at a time; today it was a full house. Sam came over to her and pulled out the first gurney. Ashleigh looked down at the orange body bag in front of her and read the tag through the transparent label pocket. *Phillips, Rose* and her date of birth. She grabbed the clipboard from Sam and looked again at the name at the top of the day's list. Ashleigh caught her breath.

Ashleigh followed the outline of Rose's body with her eyes. She reasoned that Rose Phillips wasn't a relative, not even an acquaintance – she was a neighbour, someone she'd never met or spoken to. Chewing her top lip, she silently reminded herself that she was a professional and had a job to do.

'You okay, Doc?' Sam asked, as he noticed the look on Ashleigh's face.

'Yep, I'm fine. Let's just get on with this, okay? It's going to be a long day.'

Sam rolled the gurney into the high risk suite at the far end of the room where autopsies were performed on badly decomposed bodies. Ashleigh wondered how many bags she had opened, three hundred, four hundred? She was reluctant to open the zipper at first, knowing that once she did, all the horror of death would be exposed. It was always like this. Ashleigh never knew what she would find until she mustered the courage and opened the bag, but once she did, she accepted what she was dealing with and just got on with the job. Time of death, cause of death, mechanism of death. These were the questions, she just had to find the answers.

The tang of rotting flesh escaped as Ashleigh unhooked the zipper and dragged it carefully down the length of the bag. Sam transferred the body onto the cold metallic table and set about removing and bagging the clothing. He washed the body while Ashleigh went over the day's list which now also included Mike Cole's list. When Sam was finished, Ashleigh returned to the examination table. She pushed her arms into her white lab coat, strapped her mask over her face and pulled on the pair of blue disposable gloves. She began her initial examination and pressed the button on her Dictaphone. Bacteria had already started its work on the tissues and the skin had taken on a greenish-red colour. She turned to Sam.

'She's been deceased for at least four to five days.' Maggots crawled on the outside of Rose's body and gas had already formed in the cavities and beneath the skin. She began to pick the maggots off with her gloved hand and deposited a small sample of them in a vial. She touched Rose's abdomen, the skin was splitting and leaking fluid. Ashleigh thought it ironic that she was now about to know more about Rose Phillips in death, than she would ever have known about her while she was still alive and living two doors down from her in Eden Street.

Sam began taking photos of the body. Ashleigh's lips tightened. She was silently annoyed that Rose's hands had not been bagged at the scene and sighed in resignation as she began the first part of the physical examination. Ashleigh looked over at the plastic bag and the coat that Rose's body had been wrapped in, the same woollen coat she'd been wearing the day she saw her walking up Eden Street with her shopping trolley. The timing was right. She cleared her throat and spoke in a professional and monotone voice into the Dictaphone. She stretched and tugged at the surgical gloves before she took Rose's hands in hers and lifted them gently, rubbing them as if to reassure the woman, even though her lifeless body was beyond reassurance. She examined Rose's fingernails searching for any skin or paint residue. Using an ultraviolet light, she scanned the body, searching for anything which she may have missed. Sam was taking hair and nail samples when Ashleigh sensed someone's presence behind her. Detective Senior Sergeant Nick Rimis entered the viewing room, a glass mezzanine enclosure above the autopsy room.

'How ya doing, Ash?' he said in his usual sardonic voice through the room's microphone.

'Fine, perfectly fine, Senior Sargeant,' she replied with a frown. Ashleigh tried to ignore him for as long as she could. She was annoyed by the interruption his presence had caused and didn't bother to look up at him. Instead she continued recording her observations and concentrated on the notes she had already made. She could do without interruptions right now and wondered what he was doing here. Nick Rimis always had a habit of turning up in places she wished he wouldn't. Like the time he turned up drunk at her apartment after his last girlfriend, Laura dumped him.

Frown lines surfaced on Ashleigh's forehead. They became more pronounced now as she placed her pen and clipboard down on the stainless steel counter and pulled the mask and safety glasses away from her face. She stripped her hands of her gloves and threw them with the mask in the yellow bin marked 'toxic waste'.

Rimis looked up from his newspaper when she entered the viewing room. He was reading the sports section. The Roosters were at the bottom of the league table two seasons running. 'What's up?' Rimis said, sensing something was troubling Ashleigh.

Ashleigh looked down at the body on the examination table. 'She's my neighbour, or rather, she was my neighbour.' They both looked at Rose's body. 'She lived two doors down from me.'

'I didn't know you'd moved. Why didn't you tell me? We could have had a house warming party.'

'That's exactly why I didn't tell you.'

'So who've you got down there?' Rimis tugged at his tie as if was strangling him.

'Her name's Rose Phillips.'

Rimis raised his eyebrows. 'She's one of mine. I'm working on her case.'

'So, do you want to join me? I've got a spare pair of scrubs. You can fill me in, answer any questions I might have.'

'You know I've got a sensitive stomach, Ash. I only dropped by to see if you feel like going for a drink and something to eat after work?'

Ashleigh knew Nick Rimis well enough to know that he wouldn't take no for an answer. She also knew that by the end of the day she would probably need a drink and knew he was probably the only person capable of filling her in on the missing pieces of this case.

She looked down at Rose's body. 'I should be finished here around seven. I'll meet you at Otto's, but only for a drink, okay?'

Rimis placed his hand on her arm, smiled and wondered what it was about the Phillips's case that was getting to Ashleigh. She was usually so cool and detached. Ashleigh returned to the autopsy room and Rimis returned to his newspaper. He had time to kill before meeting up with his new recruit Jill Brennan, and he hoped that she wasn't going to be as raw as he had been when he joined the unit. But he doubted it; she had acted like a real pro when he met her for the first time at the Phillips's house last Friday.

'Caucasian, female, mid eighties, grey, shoulder length hair, brown eyes, one centimetre birthmark on left cheek, scar, two and a half centimetres below her right knee, a vertical cholecystectomy scar on the abdomen, bruising on the forehead and chin, signs of poor circulation. Overall condition of the body – undernourished.' Ashleigh pulled her safety glasses on, plugged in the Stryker saw and opened the chest cavity. She lifted off the sternum and the attached ribs releasing with it a foul smelling odour of blood and offal. She placed it on the stainless steel tray and then examined the exposed lungs and heart. Systematically, she removed the organs, weighing each as she went.

'Got any big plans for tonight, Doc?' Sam asked.

'Yep, lots of paperwork,' Ashleigh lied. Sam was good at his job, a little too good. He enjoyed working with dead people, probably because they never complained. She thought he was ghoulish and wondered if he had a girlfriend. Ashleigh made an incision from behind the left ear over the crown of the head to the right ear. She examined the brain in situ and then severed the cranial nerves and spinal cord, lifted the brain gently from the skull so she could examine it further. It was a long process and Ashleigh's legs were aching. She methodically recorded her findings. She looked up at the viewing room and realised that Rimis had left. A finding of death from suicide or natural causes would make him happy she thought to herself, but a finding of homicide would not. 'Sam sew up for me and tidy up here will you? I'm going to my office.'

'Sure. No problemo.' Sam liked Ashleigh. Nothing was ever too much trouble for Doc Taylor. The whole department liked her; she was a real pro, but she took her job to heart, too much sometimes.

Chapter Eleven

Otto's bar was a dive but it was a quiet place to hang out. The patrons were mainly cops or staffers from the morgue. It was on the seedy side of town, but its patrons were used to seedy. Ashleigh pushed open the front door and looked around for Nick Rimis. Tony was here tonight playing the alto sax. Soft, soulful blues. His playing cried out to her, seduced her and suddenly she felt like crying with the loss and regret that she heard in those low notes

The bar tender was Tony's brother and he was serving tequila shots to a grey faced man who looked like he needed a friend to talk to tonight. Nick Rimis was propped up at the bar. He had his back turned away from the grey faced man and was talking to someone Ashleigh assumed was also a detective. He had that look about him, the crumpled, cheap suit he was wearing didn't sit comfortably on him, his tie had worked its way loose and the sign of a five o'clock shadow was forming on his crooked face.

Ashleigh walked up to Rimis and tapped him lightly on the shoulder. 'Buy a girl a drink?' she said.

He spun around, stood up and pecked her lightly on each cheek, the way Europeans do. 'What are ya having, Ash?'

'Make it a white wine, something cold and dry will do.' She looked at the guy who'd been talking to Rimis when she came through the door.

'I'm Colin. I work with this guy,' he pointed at Rimis with his thumb and laughed. He took Ashleigh's hand in his, shook it hard and gave her the once over. He dipped his thick, pudgy fingers into the plastic bowl of mixed nuts which were sitting on the bar. Ashleigh watched him as he licked his fingers and decided she'd give the nuts a miss.

Rimis ordered a round of drinks and when they arrived, Ashleigh threw back a large mouthful and swallowed hard. The liquid coated the back of her throat; it was refreshing, like when you dive into a pool after a stinking hot, dusty summer's day. Both Rimis and Ashleigh ignored Colin and he soon got the hint. He picked up his beer and walked down to the far end of the bar.

'The Phillips's case turn up anything interesting?' Rimis asked.

'Nothing obvious, or nothing I wouldn't have expected from a woman her age. She was undernourished, had a few circulation problems, but considering her age and the fact that she was living on her own, I'm not really surprised. There was also a bit of bruising on her face possibly from when her face hit the table after she passed out. I'm waiting for the tox reports and the drug and alcohol screens to come in before I type up my report. Should be in the next day or two.' Ashleigh looked at Rimis and took another mouthful of wine.

'What's wrong Ash? I know that look.'

'What look?'

'The one you get when you've got something bugging you.'

Ashleigh swirled the remainder of her wine around the bottom of the glass and held the stem with her thumb and index finger. 'Look, I didn't really know Rose Phillips, okay, but I'd seen her, heard the talk from the neighbours.'

Rimis raised his eyebrows.

'I know your take on all of this. You think it was suicide don't you?'

Rimis looked at her, took a slug of beer and let her continue.

'The police report said that a real estate agent found her body and that they found sleeping tablets, antidepressants and Scotch at the scene. Well, here's a bit of information you might not know. The house is already on the market. Big sign, I'm surprised that it hasn't got bright neon lights flashing on top. There's a 'deceased estate' sticker slapped right across the middle of it. I'm thinking, what if the son has money problems. I hear he has a fancy lifestyle and a demanding wife. What if he wanted Rose out of the way so he could sell the house? Kevin told me Rose was a stubborn, proud woman. What if she wanted to stay put, didn't want to cooperate? I'm sorry, Nick, but suicide just doesn't seem to fit the profile and she didn't seem the type to be a heavy drinker either. There were no signs of alcohol abuse, her liver was in good shape considering her age. Anyway, it'll be interesting to see the results when they come back and what her alcohol reading was at the time of death.'

'Look Ash, we're still treating this case as suicide, there's no real evidence to think otherwise. You gotta remember, sometimes alcohol helps beats the blues and any other worries you might have, especially when you're old and nobody gives a shit.'

'Sounds like you're talking from experience Nicko.'

Rimis looked down at his empty glass and quickly changed the subject. 'By the way, have you heard the son's asked the Coroner for an inquest? Like you, he seems to think the old lady didn't top herself.'

'That's interesting. Well, he has the right to do that, Nick, but it's up to the Coroner whether he thinks an inquest is warranted, you know that.'

'Let me know when you've finished your report.'

They sat and listened to the music and didn't say anything to each other for sometime before Ashleigh spoke. 'Kevin Taggart has offered to drive me and the old women who live across the street, to the funeral. Might be interesting to see who turns up and check out what the family's like.'

'I'll go along as well and I'll bring the rookie for experience. She's bright and a good looker. Her name's Brennan, Jill Brennan.' Rimis finished his beer. 'Your shout mate,' he called out to Colin at the other end of the bar. 'I'll have the same again.' He turned to Ashleigh, 'What about you Ash, want another one?'

She shook her head. 'No thanks, I have to drive.'

'Anyway, as I was saying,' Rimis continued, 'Jill

Brennan, she's been in the force for about four years now and she's interested in this case for some reason. I suppose it's because she was the one who broke the news to the son. He took it hard apparently.'

'Listen Nick, forget Brennan for a minute will you, and do me a favour. Apart from the son, you might want to do a bit of digging around, find out about my neighbour, Kevin Taggart. There's something odd about him that just doesn't sit right with me. He seems to have an unhealthy fascination for little old ladies, always going on about how proud and lonely they are and the trouble that causes.'

'I interviewed him when I was there last Friday. I know what you mean about him, but he's an artist, maybe he's just eccentric.'

Ashleigh shrugged her shoulders and looked at her watch.

'Want to come for something to eat?' Rimis asked, as Ashleigh searched her shoulder bag and pulled out a twenty-dollar note from her purse for the next round of drinks.

'Nick, I'm really beat. I'm going home for an early night. Nice meeting you Colin,' she called out and waved in his direction.

'Yeah, likewise. I'm sure I'll run into you again sometime, bound to, in our line of work,' Colin laughed and raised his glass. He had his arms around Stephanie Brooks, a legal clerk from the Coroner's office.

Ashleigh walked out onto the busy street and wrapped her coat around her. The nights were turning cold.

Chapter Twelve

Frederick Milne took two steps at a time and entered the foyer of the Glebe Coroners' Court. Forty-five minutes later, he entered the court room carrying a large clutch of case files under his arm, sat down and made himself comfortable in a worn leather chair. The Coroner was not a big man nor was he powerfully built. His neatly trimmed moustache was peppered with the first signs of grey which looked at odds with his jet black hair. He looked insignificant as he scratched his chin and examined the files sitting on the desk in front of him. Jane Fairchild, the Coronial Advocate assisting him, stood and looked out at the expectant faces of the small group of people gathered before her in the courtroom. She made an opening address and outlined the background of the case and the issues to be investigated. Milne looked up and addressed the court.

'This is the inquest into the death of Rose Patricia Phillips. Before we start, I'll ask if there are any members of Rose Phillips's family present here this morning?'

William raised his hand and stood up. 'Yes, Your Worship, I'm William Phillips, Rose Phillips's son.'

'Good morning Mr Phillips. I'm sorry we meet in these circumstances. I know you may have a number of questions you may wish to ask today and we will try to do our best to provide you with the answers. Can I ask if you have anyone representing you?'

'No, Your Worship.'

Frederick Milne nodded and asked William if he had seen a copy of the brief and the evidence that was to be presented.

'I have Your Worship.'

Jill Brennan didn't look at William when she was called to take the stand. She focused on the Coroner as she walked towards the front of the courtroom and missed the look William gave her.

'Please tell the court your name, rank and station.'

'My name is Jillian Margaret Brennan. I am a Senior Constable of police and currently stationed with the Serious Crime Investigation Unit.'

'Were you rostered to be on duty on Friday, the 22nd May of this year, Senior Constable?'

'Yes, I was.'

'Did you receive a communication to attend at number 15 Eden Street on that day?'

'I did.'

'And did you go there?'

'Yes, I attended the scene.'

'Were you accompanied by another officer and if so what was that officer's name?'

'I was accompanied by Constable Daniel French.'

'What did you see when you arrived at the scene?'

'We spoke to a Miss Ambah St John, a real estate agent who had called in a death. Miss St John advised us that she had been commissioned to sell the house by the deceased's daughter-in-law, a Mrs Suellyn Phillips. Constable French and I were directed to the side of the house. She advised us that the occupant was in the kitchen and appeared deceased. Constable French being taller than myself looked through the kitchen window first and it did appear to him that she was deceased.'

'Can you please describe the deceased?'

'The deceased was wearing a grey coat and from the condition in which we found her, she appeared to have been deceased for some days. The deceased was face down on the table and her arms were hanging by her side. There were two empty packets of prescription medication on the table, Sinequan and Noctamid. There was also an empty bottle of Scotch and an empty jam jar on the kitchen drainer. Mrs Phillips's cat was locked in the laundry.'

'From the observations you've just described, were you able to come to any conclusion or opinion what had caused the deceased's death?'

'We came to the conclusion that she had taken her own life. A mixture of alcohol and prescription drugs seemed to be the likely cause.'

William buried his head in his hands and shook his head.

'Constable French and I notified the deceased's son, Mr William Phillips at approximately eleven-fifteen am on Friday morning, the 22nd May.' Jill looked in William's direction. 'I also contacted...' Jill looked at her notebook, 'Doctor Mark Fitzgerald to arrange for the provision of medical records pertaining to the deceased. Doctor Fitzgerald is a general practitioner at the Medical Centre in Riverview. He informed me that he had been the deceased's doctor for several years and considered that until the time of her death, in general terms, she had been in a state of good physical health. He informed us that he had last examined the deceased approximately seven months prior when she had presented with depression and insomnia. It was at this time that he prescribed Sinequan and Noctamid.'

'Did you carry out any other form of investigation?'

'I did. At approximately six pm on Monday the 25th May, I attended the Glebe Morgue where the post mortem was being carried out on the deceased. I spoke with a Doctor Ashleigh Taylor who was performing the procedure at the time. She informed me that she was waiting on toxicology reports before making her findings, but at that stage there didn't appear to be any evidence of foul play.'

'So, in terms of the police investigation...?'

'In my opinion there were no suspicious circumstances surrounding the deceased's death. I believed at the time after speaking with Miss St John that the stress of moving to a retirement village and having to leave her home may have been the impetus for her to take her own life.'

'Was a suicide note of any kind found at the scene?'

'No, there wasn't.'

'Thank you Senior Constable, I have no further

questions for you. Mr Phillips is there any information you wish to know or any other questions you wish to ask Senior Constable Brennan?'

'Yes, your Worship. I'd like to ask what the name of the Scotch was that was found at the scene?'

'I believe it was *Highland Park*,' Brennan replied.

If that's all?' Frederick Milne raised his head and looked at William.

William nodded.

'Thank you Senior Constable, you may step down.'

Jill Brennan didn't look at William as she walked past him and returned to her seat at the rear of the court.

'Your Worship, I would like to call Doctor Ashleigh Taylor,' Jane Fairchild said.

Ashleigh took the stand, crossed her bare legs and adjusted her skirt.

'Please tell the court your full name and current occupation.'

Ashleigh cleared her throat. 'My name is Doctor Ashleigh Louise Taylor. I am a forensic pathologist employed by New South Wales Health and Pathology and am contracted to supply forensic services to the Coroner.

'I believe you conducted an autopsy on the body of Rose Patricia Phillips on Monday, the 25th May this year?'

'Yes, that's correct.'

After Ashleigh presented her findings and the results of the toxicology report to the Court, Jane Fairchild stood and faced the Coroner. 'That's all the evidence we propose to lead for the purpose of Your Worship making a preliminary finding in the inquest of Mrs Rose Phillips under section 53 of the Coroners' Act.'

'Do you wish to ask Doctor Taylor any questions Mr Phillips?' the Coroner asked.

'Yes, Your Worship,' William replied. He stood and buttoned his jacket, shuffled his feet and looked across at Ashleigh. 'Doctor Taylor, the bruising on my mother's face. I was wondering about that. Is it possible to tell what caused this bruising and did you find any evidence to suggest that it was not self-inflicted?'

'To answer your question Mr Phillips, can I first say that bruises as a rule are simple injuries. The interpretation of bruising on a body is different in every person because people bruise at different rates. Also bruising continues a short time after death. As we all know, as people age, the skin becomes thinner. This is because the blood vessels are less protected from injury as the circulatory system undergoes pathological changes. An injury inflicted by mild trauma, for example, bumping one's head against a table may result in a substantial bruise. The site of the bruising was consistent with your mother's face coming into contact with the kitchen table. Her nose and chin were badly bruised but I found no evidence to suggest any homicidal bruising. I also found no evidence of bruising on the neck or any finger or nail marks to indicate that a hand had been used to produce the bruising. I hope this answers your question, Mr Phillips.'

'Thank you,' William said.

There was a short recess so Coroner Milne could prepare his findings. On his return to the Court forty minutes later, Frederick Milne put his reading glasses on and looked at William Phillips. 'The finding of this Court is this: that Rose Patricia Phillips died somewhere between the hours of four-thirty p.m. and six pm on Wednesday, the 20th of May at her home at 15 Eden Street, Lane Cove in the state of New South Wales and that the cause of death was a combination of alcohol and prescription drugs. She suffered from sleep apnea, a sleeping disorder that caused her to take sleeping medication on the afternoon she died as well as Sinequan, an antidepressant drug. The manner of death is undetermined. The death can now be registered and the body released for burial. I express my sympathy to you and to your family on your loss, Mr Phillips.'

There was a scurry of activity, Milne stood and gathered his papers, chairs shifted and scraped on the timber floor, doors closed.

'Thank you, Your Worship' was all that William said. He stood and left the court room. He pulled his coat closer to his body and grabbed his keys from his pocket. As he aimed the remote control at his car, the blip of the unlock button was lost to the wind. He opened the driver's door at the same time as a woman's voice called his name. Her voice was strong and clear. He inserted the key in the ignition and stood by the car resting his arm on the top of the opened driver's door.

'William,' Jill was short of breath. I'm glad I caught up with you before you left.' She touched his arm lightly, 'I'm sorry you had to go through all of that and that you didn't get the answers you were looking for.' She turned her head back towards the direction of the Court.

'Thanks Jill, thanks for everything. I'll give you a

call, but now's not a good time.' He wasn't sure what he was going to do about Jill Brennan or what Jill Brennan was going to do about him.

William pulled up outside his mother's house in Eden Street and looked through the windscreen at the 'For Sale' sign planted in her front yard. A diesel motor hummed behind him and his eyes darted to the rear view mirror. A silver-grey Landcruiser turned into a neighbouring driveway. He knew the pathologist who performed the autopsy on his mother was a neighbour and he watched as the Landcruiser came to a stop and Ashleigh Taylor stepped down from the vehicle.

William opened the car door and walked up the uneven footpath towards her. Ashleigh was standing by the letter box flicking through her mail. She looked up and recognised William Phillips immediately.

'Hello, Mr Phillips.'

'Hello Doctor Taylor, I hope you don't mind me coming here like this.' He turned and looked back at his mother's house. 'I came to take a look at my mother's house, then I saw you pull up and...'

'No, that's okay. I understand. Today must have been tough on you.'

William nodded and rubbed the knot at the back of his neck.

'You look like you've got something on your mind.'

'Well, I have as a matter of fact.'

'Better we talk inside than stand out here on the footpath... the neighbours...' she nodded in the direction of the Blake house where Edi Blake was standing in the front yard watering the garden.

William smiled as he looked behind at Edi Blake. Rose had told him about the Blake sisters when she first arrived in Eden Street and how friendly they had been towards her. He was surprised that they were still alive.

Ashleigh unlocked the front door and William followed her down the timber hallway through the galley kitchen. She opened the back sliding door and showed him out onto the covered deck. The smell of freshly cut grass drifted up from the backyard.

'Red wine okay?'

'Sounds good, thanks.'

Ashleigh carried the bottle to the table and poured the wine into two glasses.

'Well, fire away, what would you like to know?' Ashleigh took a sip of wine and looked at him. She remembered what she had said to Rimis about him having a motive. William Phillips didn't look like the type who was capable of murder and she realised that she may have misjudged him. Ashleigh looked hard into his dark eyes and could see the confusion in them. He looked like he hadn't slept for days. He was unshaven, but after looking beneath the haggard, tired face she could see that he was a good looking man with a strong jawline and a warm open face. He had thin lips and a perfect set of teeth, no doubt a result of expensive dental work.

'Ashleigh, there's something that's been troubling

me with this whole terrible business. I wanted to ask you about my mother's blood alcohol reading. It was high wasn't it? Zero point two-one, you said in your report.'

'Yes, from memory, that's right. To be honest, I was quite surprised, but as I said in Court, when alcohol is combined with a drug like Sinequan as it was in this case, a more intoxicated state can occur and if your mother was drinking just before she died, then the level would be higher than if she had stopped drinking say, a few hours beforehand. The combination of Sinequan and alcohol in these proportions can cause excessive sedation and eventually, death. She had also taken Noctamid, a prescription drug used for sleep apnea on the afternoon that she died.'

'The problem I have reconciling all of this in my mind is that my mother never drank. She was a tee-totaller all her life. I never knew her to drink alcohol, she wouldn't touch the stuff, not even at my wedding. Her father had a history of alcohol abuse and violence against her mother. One smell of it and it would mess with her head.'

'The police report said they found empty beer bottles at the side of the house.'

'Ginger beer. She went through a stage years ago of making her own.'

'Oh, I see.' Ashleigh nodded and realised that in her line of business it never pays to make assumptions.

'What's bothering me is that if you are going to commit suicide why would you bother to get up from the table and rinse your glass and an empty bottle and then leave them both to drain on the kitchen sink? Does that make any sense to you?'

'Well, I must admit it does sound a bit odd but she was an old lady and old habits die hard.'

'The way my mother's did.'

Ashleigh looked at William and saw something written on his face. Guilt or sadness or perhaps it was both. 'William, I've seen cases where some people go to extremes to clean up after themselves, not wanting to leave a mess behind for their loved ones to have to deal with.' They were quiet for a moment before Ashleigh asked what he knew about Kevin Taggart.

'Not a lot,' he replied. 'A bit of a loner I gather, but according to my wife Suellyn, he did help my mother out from time to time. He invited her in for cups of tea but I don't think she ever took him up on his offer. I know that he tried to sell her some of his paintings a few years back but she didn't buy any of his work, even though I think she felt sorry for him.'

'I know you don't think your mother committed suicide but sometimes especially when you are old and...'

'I just can't believe that she would do something like that. To take her own life is just so out of character. She was such a proud woman.'

'What, so if you don't think she committed suicide, do you think she was murdered?'

'That's the problem. Who would want to kill her and why? The police seem to think that all the evidence and especially your report, support the idea that it was suicide or at least an accidental combination of alcohol and drugs. She was a proud and stubborn old woman who kept to herself. I didn't know what was going on in her life, I'm ashamed to say. When I heard that she was taking antidepressants I was really surprised. The only thing I can think of is that she could have started taking the antidepressants because of the thought of having to leave the house and having to move to a retirement village. I don't really know how long my wife had been pestering her to move out of the house. Maybe that was enough reason to drive her to drink. But, then again, why not simply overdose. I just think there has got to be something more to all of this, my legal mind tells me that *there is* more to this.'

William sighed and looked down at his hands. 'I blame my wife for all this.' He drained his glass. As he placed it on the table he thought of the jam jars in his mother's kitchen and felt ashamed. Ashamed of himself for not knowing about the life his mother had been living while he sat back in his beachside apartment, drinking expensive wine from crystal glasses. He stood up and slid his chair back from the table. 'Thanks for hearing me out Ashleigh and for handling my mother's autopsy so sensitively. It's some job you've got.' William wondered how she could stand dealing with the dead every day, wondered how she coped.

Ashleigh led William up the hallway to the front door. 'If you have any more questions you know where to find me.'

After William left, Ashleigh leant against the closed door. She shut her eyes tightly, thought of Rose, then thought of her grandmother. It was two years ago to the day that she had found her floating in the bath tub. She had been dead for a week.

Chapter Thirteen

Kevin Taggart sat down with a steaming cup of coffee and the morning newspaper. He had the habit of reading the paper in a particular order, turning first to the death notices and then to the sports' section. He looked quickly down the list of funeral notices and smiled when he saw her name.

'PHILLIPS, Rose Patricia (née Evans). Family and friends are warmly invited to attend a Memorial Service for the late Mrs Rose PHILLIPS to be held at St Benedict's Church, Victoria Road, Ultimo, at noon on Wednesday…'

He read the notice again. St Benedict's. What a coincidence. Every Sunday as a child he worshipped there without fail. Even if he was ill, his mother never let him miss Sunday Mass at St Benedict's.

It was an overcast and drizzly Wednesday morning. Flashes of lightning lit the sky and an occasional clap of thunder was heard in the distance. Appropriate weather for a funeral, Kevin thought as he buttoned a clean shirt and tightened the belt of the only decent pair of trousers he owned. As he reached for his tie he knew that it was the wrong colour and the wrong shape. It had gone out of fashion years ago. Looking at his reflection in the mirror he combed a few greasy strands of his hair, which refused to lie flat, against his skull.

He turned the ignition over twice before he put the small, yellow sedan into gear and leant on the horn to let Ashleigh know it was time to leave. But he needn't have bothered. Ashleigh and the sisters were waiting for him at the top of the driveway. 'What a merry outing this is going to be,' Kevin chuckled.

Ashleigh settled herself into the passenger seat and Kevin opened the rear doors for Rhoda and Edi. He made sure they were comfortable and their seat belts were fastened tight before locking the doors.

The Blake sisters were dressed in black outfits, as was appropriate. Rhoda looked smart in a black pillbox hat veiled in black netting which draped softly over her forehead. Kevin imagined that the hat had been sitting on top of her wardrobe for years in a dusty hat box, waiting for just such an occasion.

Edi and Rhoda sat looking out at the traffic through the foggy side windows and listened to the rhythmic brush of the rubber wipers as they stroked the windscreen. Ashleigh noticed the seat covers were ripped and frayed at the edges as she hummed along softly to the classical music as it played quietly in the background. The traffic was heavy and Kevin darted and weaved his way through the city. He slammed on the brakes and hammered the horn as a truck suddenly changed lanes in front of him.

'Bloody idiot, get out of the way,' he yelled, then remembered the sisters in the back seat. 'Sorry ladies, please excuse my language, but there are some people on the road who don't deserve to have a driver's licence.' The sisters didn't say a word.

On the other side of town, William Phillips called out to his wife as he brushed away a piece of stray hair which had fallen onto the lapel of his jacket. 'Hurry up Suellyn, what are you doing? I don't want to be late for the funeral.'

Suellyn applied the last of her makeup and looked in the full-length mirror on the dressing room wall, tilted her head and was satisfied. 'I'm coming. But I can't find my black leather handbag, the one with the gold chain. You haven't seen it have you, William?'

William didn't know where her handbag was and wasn't about to help her find it. 'I'll be waiting in the car.' He grabbed the car keys and walked towards the lift. He checked his watch and wondered why it mattered so much to Suellyn that she had to have that particular bag. She must have at least ten other black bags to choose from. And to be late today, today of all days. William fumed. He just knew the traffic was going to be chaotic as he opened the car door and slumped behind the steering wheel.

Suellyn finally appeared and eased herself into

the leather passenger seat. She turned towards William and patted his knee. 'Found it,' she said and placed her gold chained handbag on her lap. She didn't notice William roll his eyes as he reversed the Mercedes out of the parking bay and drove out through the basement garage into the heavy rain.

'It's all right William, calm down. I don't know why you're getting yourself so upset. They won't start the service without us. We're family.'

They travelled the eleven kilometres to the city through the rain in silence.

'Park there, William, next to that old yellow car.' Suellyn pointed to the vacant space in the church car park. The rain had eased and they entered St Benedict's through the sandstone block archway.

William and Suellyn were escorted by a funeral attendant to a pew in the second row on the right hand side of the church. They shuffled past an elderly woman deep in prayer wearing a ridiculous hat. A spotted grey feather poked out from beneath the band and brushed against Suellyn as she took her place on the pew. William's knees knocked against the pew in front of him. They both turned to look at the woman beside them and realised they had no idea who she was.

The woman with the feathered hat began to snore lightly; it was sleep that had overtaken her, not grief. Her head fell forward and then suddenly jerked upwards as people do when they realise that they have fallen asleep at an inappropriate time. The woman adjusted her hat and looked at William and Suellyn sympathetically. William wondered if she recognised them or perhaps she felt she already knew them from a description Rose may have given her of her only son and his wife.

The elegant arrangement of red roses William had ordered rested in the middle of the polished mahogany coffin. Roses, William remembered, were his mother's favourite flower. Suellyn nudged William in the ribs as he fiddled with his cuff links. She leant forward and picked up a hymn book from the shelf in front of her and flicked through the pages. William glanced up at a stained glass window depicting the resurrection of Christ and then turned his eyes towards the unknown woman who sat beside him. She looked away and blew her nose loudly into a man-sized handkerchief.

A black suited figure came forward and placed a bouquet of cheap, grocer shop flowers, wrapped in clear cellophane, on top of the coffin. The bundle of flowers was tied with a pink ribbon. He paused for a moment and muttered something under his breath. Tommy Dwyer turned around slowly and their eyes met - Suellyn bit her lip. Her stomach tightened as he walked past her and returned to his place at the rear of the church. William was looking down at the carpeted floor when the organ stopped playing and the small group of mourners fell silent. Father John stood up from his invisible chair behind the pulpit and addressed the congregation. The service began.

'Our sister, Rose Patricia Phillips, has died. We gather to give praise and thanks to God as we honour her life.'

William shifted in his seat and looked over his shoulder. He looked at the small congregation and realised that he didn't recognise anyone, apart from Anita, his personal assistant, who was sobbing three pews behind him. What was she doing here? She must be angling for a pay rise, he thought cynically.

The service was going on for far too long. Suellyn was grateful that William had decided not to give a eulogy. She stirred uncomfortably in her seat and placed the crumpled service sheet down beside her and looked back over her shoulder, scanning the congregation, searching for Tommy. He was sitting at the back of the church between Max Gray, Rose's gardener and an elderly man with a snowy white moustache and pouchy eyes. What was Tommy doing here? She had told him not to come. The last thing she wanted was for William to come face to face with Tommy Dwyer. She hoped there wasn't going to be a scene and prayed that he had enough sense to just slip away quietly after the service.

'Into your hands, God of mercies, we commend our sister, Rose Patricia Phillips in the sure and certain hope that together with all who have died in Christ, she will rise with him on the last day. We give you thanks for the blessings, which you have bestowed upon her in life: they are signs to us of your goodness and of our union with the saints in Christ. Grant her eternal rest.

Amen!

In peace let us take our sister, Rose Patricia Phillips, to her final place of rest.'

Tommy stood well back from the graveside. Edi was inconsolable, she thought it was her mother they were burying. Rhoda looked at Kevin as if they both realised they had made a mistake in bringing her. Ashleigh attempted to comfort Edi by holding her hand but her attention was drawn away from her when she noticed a well dressed man in his sixties who looked remarkably like William Phillips.

She turned her gaze to the woman who was holding William's arm. Suellyn Phillips was supporting him, playing the role of devoted wife. She watched as she dabbed at tears with a snowy, white tissue and shifted from one foot to the other. Suellyn looked divine in black and her long legs were accentuated by the tailored pants she was wearing.Rimis was observing everyone quietly in the background, making his own observations and winked as he met Ashleigh's eyes.

The coffin was lowered carefully and respectfully into the ground. Father John offered the final ritual, the rite of committal and the small group of mourners hurried back to their cars to escape the rain.

It was still drizzling. Kevin approached the grave and looked down into the dark, deep hole in the ground at the clumps of soil and the soggy flower stems covering the coffin. Ashleigh gently ushered the sisters back to where the car was parked. Rimis walked towards Kevin and stood across from him on the opposite side of the grave. He couldn't help but notice his out of date suit and outrageous tie. 'We're watching you, Kevin,' he whispered.

Kevin blinked twice and stuttered, 'I have to go. The ladies are waiting for me.'

'Maybe you can give me a call sometime, Kevin. I'd like to see your paintings. I'm a bit of an artist myself.' Rimis reached into the inside pocket of his suit jacket and opened his wallet. He pulled out a creased business card and walked over to where Kevin was standing and stuffed it into the breast pocket of his suit jacket. Kevin nodded nervously and hurried off towards the car park.

Tommy decided it was proper to offer his condolences even though it was raining and he had a long way to drive home. Suellyn watched him striding towards them and tried to work out his mood from the look on his face, but it was impossible; his face was flat and free from emotion. He was holding a large, black umbrella above his head, his shoulders were hunched and she worried that he might slip as he sidestepped a muddy puddle of water as he approached their parked car.

William held the car door open for Suellyn and juggled his umbrella over her head to protect her from the drizzle, which looked as if it would turn into a downpour at any moment.

Tommy approached the car and extended his hand. 'My condolences to you both.'

The rims of their umbrellas bumped against each other and sparked off a shower of rain drops. With the two men standing side-by-side, their similarities were obvious and impossible to ignore, the same dark eyes, the same thin lips, the same height. Suellyn wondered if they could see the similarities in the other, if they could see what she could see. But if William had noticed the likeness, he wasn't about to say anything.

'Thanks for coming today, especially in such miserable weather.' William shook Tommy's hand firmly. 'Did you know my mother from Eden Street?' he asked politely, even though he was annoyed at having to stand in the rain and speak to this stranger. They were all getting drenched. William looked at Tommy, thinking he looked familiar. Tommy looked at William and thought the same.

'Pleased to meet you, sorry it's under such sad circumstances. Your mother and I go back a long way,' he said, as a large raindrop dripped from his umbrella and ran down the back of his neck.

'Well, Suellyn and I certainly appreciate you coming. My mother didn't have many friends, at least that I know of.' William looked at Suellyn and noticed her face was pale and drawn. The stress from Rose's death was obviously getting to her. He felt guilty now as he realised that he had underestimated the feelings Suellyn had for his mother. He had no idea that she cared so much. 'Let's get going Suellyn, let's get out of this rain.' Suellyn didn't take her eyes off Tommy as she edged her way into the car and settled into the passenger seat.

'Nice to meet you both.' Tommy gave a quick wave but didn't make any attempt to move from where he was standing. He stood his ground as the rain grew heavier and water seeped into his shoes. His eyes followed the Mercedes as it reversed out of the angled car space and drove off slowly down the road. A new set of mourners were arriving. Dealing with the dead was big business he thought as he turned and walked back towards his car.

Kevin was losing his patience. The traffic was at a standstill. Torrential rain punched the car's roof and a flash of lightning raced across the sky in the distance. Edi sobbed uncontrollably in the back seat and cascades of water ran in torrents down the face of the windscreen.

'Poor Rose. Not much of a send off, not even a wake,' Rhoda said as she wiped her eyes and blew her nose into a handkerchief. 'I had at least expected a glass of sherry, didn't you Edi?' Edi's blank eyes were transfixed by the traffic filing past the passenger window and she didn't answer her sister.

'You can be comforted in knowing that she's at peace now Rhoda.' Kevin looked in the rear view mirror at the sisters and mumbled, 'Pride, the never failing vice of fools.' He looked across at Ashleigh then turned his attentions to the car in front. He pumped the horn. The wiper blades scraped the windscreen and the sudden downpour flooded the blocked gutters sending water gushing across the road in torrents.

Chapter Fourteen

William and Suellyn sat across from Martin Bartholomew. His desk was piled high with manila folders secured by faded red cotton tape. The only window in the first floor office looked out onto the busy street below. A coffee mug sat next to an empty ash tray and as Suellyn shifted in her seat, her eyes were drawn to the specks of dandruff on Martin Bartholomew's cardigan and noticed his frayed shirt collar which was too tight for his thick neck.

'Now where was I?' Bartholomew directed the question more to himself than to the couple sitting in front of him. 'Ah, yes. But before we begin, can I first offer my condolences? Mrs Phillips senior was a very fine woman. I had become quite fond of her over the years.' Bartholomew wiped a rogue tear from the corner of his eye. 'Well, on to business, let's get on with it shall we?' Bartholomew's mood suddenly brightened as he sorted through the files on his desk. Here it is, the last will and testament of Rose Patricia Phillips or Evans as she was formally known. She changed her name to Phillips by deed poll, did you know that Mr Phillips?'

'To be honest, no, I didn't.' William was genuinely surprised. He looked across at the insignificant little man sitting behind his timber veneer desk and wondered why his mother had chosen him to act as the executor to her estate. 'Let's get on with it then Bartholomew, what's in this will? I can't imagine there's much to get too excited about.' William looked at his watch. He had a midday lunch appointment in the city and knew he would be late if they didn't get this over and done with quickly.

'Well, you might be surprised. In fact William...' Bartholomew paused for a moment and looked at his client's son. 'I can call you William, can't I?'

William couldn't believe that his mother's solicitor was so pompous and so old-fashioned. He was surprised when he had insisted that they come to his suburban office to read Rose's will. 'Of course. Let's just get on with it.'

Martin Bartholomew smiled and continued. 'Your mother was a wealthy woman in her own right. There is actually quite a substantial estate.' Suellyn stopped looking out the window, turned and faced William and then transferred her gaze to Bartholomew. She urged him with her eyes to continue. The fine hairs on the back of Suellyn's neck stood on end.

Mr Martin Bartholomew of Bartholomew and Smyth, Solicitors, opened the file and handed copies of Rose's will to Suellyn and William. 'Let's begin then shall we?' He cleared his throat. 'This is the last will and testament of Rose Phillips... To my next door neighbour Mr Kevin Taggart, I bequeath three hundred thousand dollars to assist him in the pursuit of his artistic endeavours and to my friend Max Gray, I bequeath twenty thousand dollars for his kindness and friendship.'

Suellyn and William looked at each other in disbelief, then looked back at Bartholomew. 'You've got to be kidding,' Suellyn moaned, rolled her eyes and shook her head in disbelief.

'The remainder of my estate,' Bartholomew paused solely for effect, 'I bequeath to William Seymour Phillips and Thomas Seymour Dwyer, to be divided equally.'

'Who the hell is Thomas Dwyer?' William looked at Bartholomew, searching his eyes for an answer.

Bartholomew ignored William's question and peered over his glasses and looked at Suellyn as she sat rigid in the chair, her eyes glazed, she was visibly shaken. But he was only mildly concerned. He had seen this sort of thing before. 'Are you all right, Mrs Phillips? Can I get you a glass of water?'

Suellyn ignored his question and William waved his hand by way of a dismissal.

The solicitor returned to the document and continued. 'To answer your question William, Thomas Dwyer is the son of the late Mrs Isabelle Dwyer. Mrs Dwyer and your mother had a special friendship which spanned many decades.' Bartholomew scratched his chin, drawing them out, sensing their excitement and anticipation.

'Now, regarding the value of the remainder of the estate, I would estimate, once the shares are sold and brokerage fees, funeral costs, commissions and stamp duties have been taken into account, we are looking at around the ten and a half million dollar mark.'

'Good Lord,' William gasped. 'How did my mother end up with that sort of money?' Suellyn rubbed her arm nervously, crossed and uncrossed her legs. She looked pale and Bartholomew thought she had the look about her as if she was about to faint.

'Are you sure I can't get you a glass of water, Mrs Phillips?' he asked almost too kindly.

Suellyn shook her head. She didn't want to take the risk of picking up any infectious diseases.

Bartholomew took his wired glasses from his face and leant forward on his elbows. He placed his fists on his chin and looked across the desk at William and Suellyn, sighed in a judgmental sort of way and began to explain how Rose had inherited money from a Miss Dora Valentine when she died and also received a considerable amount of money from the estate of a Mrs Isabelle Dwyer six months ago. Rose invested the funds in the share market, and wisely, so it seemed. 'When Mrs Phillips came in to sign her will, she told me she spent at least four hours a week at the Council library where she had access to a community computer. Afterwards she would pick up a few groceries at the local supermarket before heading home.' Bartholomew smiled to himself. He loved the drama of will readings, especially when the beneficiaries didn't have the faintest idea what was in them.

Suellyn and William couldn't wait to leave Bartholomew's office. They thanked him for his time, grabbed a copy of Rose's will and left. Suellyn followed William down the uncarpeted flight of stairs to the dingy foyer. In his haste to get out of the building, William tugged at the door and pulled it towards him. Suellyn brushed past him and pushed the door open.

William's face was ashen. 'Let's have coffee,' he called out to Suellyn as she walked off in front of him, heading back towards the Council car park.

Suellyn stopped and spun around in surprise. 'What about your lunch appointment in the city?'

'There's a lot we need to talk about. I need some time to think this through, to look more closely at this will. There are things in it that just don't add up and don't make sense.'

They waited together on the footpath for the traffic lights to change but William was impatient. He grabbed Suellyn by the elbow and dragged her across the pedestrian crossing. They passed the Council library and an Indian takeaway, the distinctive smell of curry and fried samosas reminded William that it was almost lunchtime and he'd not eaten breakfast. They walked past a coffee shop and decided on a table inside. The outside tables were all taken, filled with mothers drinking coffee and their toddlers slurping babycinos. They decided on a table near the front door and William hung his jacket on the back of the chair and ordered a short black and two slices of toasted, banana bread. Suellyn ordered a skimmed latté.

Suellyn rested her wrists on the table, placed her handbag on her lap and turned and looked behind her. Apart from a young couple sitting in the back corner next to the coffee machine and the cash register, they were the only customers inside the café. Suellyn fiddled with one of the sugar sachets, which poked up from a glass sugar bowl, she bent and twisted it. It broke and the contents spilled out onto the table. She brushed the grains into a pile with the side of her hand and was still holding the empty paper sachet when William grabbed both her hands and looked into her eyes.

'Suellyn,' William took a sudden breath. 'Look at me. Tell me what's going on. Who is this Thomas Dwyer? Did Rose ever mention his name to you?'

She pulled her hands away from his and sat back in her chair.

'You'd think the solicitor would know, after all, he drew up the will. And what was this Thomas Dwyer's relationship with my mother? She never mentioned his name to me, at least not that I can remember. Thomas Dwyer, Thomas Dwyer… the name is familiar for some reason. Hang on, wasn't he the guy who spoke to us after the funeral?'

William thought back to the day of his mother's funeral. Tommy, his name was Tommy, and William remembered the bumping of black umbrellas, drips of rain, getting wet and thinking that he somehow looked familiar, as if he had met him before.

Suellyn was thinking her own thoughts. She had no idea it would turn out this way. What was Rose doing leaving half of her estate to Tommy. She wondered if he had known about the contents of Rose's will. 'William, we really need to go through the house in Eden Street and sell it as soon as we can. The agent says that presentation is everything in this market.

Ambah also told me that she hasn't had much interest in the house, especially because your mother decided to die in the kitchen. That can apparently put some buyers off.'

'Slow down will you Suellyn, what's all this business about selling the house. I've seen the sign, you didn't waste anytime did you? How can you even think about selling it? It's not as if my mother died from some long-term illness. Everyone apart from me seems to think that she committed suicide. And if that isn't enough, she also decided to include her whacko neighbour and a complete stranger in her will, someone who just happens to share the same middle name as me. And you're talking about selling the house?' William was incredulous. Suellyn didn't like the direction the conversation was heading.

'Come on Suellyn, tell me something, will you? Why did you disconnect the power to the house? Didn't you have any idea of what effect that would have on her?' He looked at Suellyn's face and didn't like what he read in her eyes. 'But maybe you did? I can't understand why you did it, what were you trying to achieve?'

'How did you find out about the power?' Suellyn asked, with surprise.

'The police told me. You must have known that I'd find out sooner or later?'

'It's my house William, you bought it in my name remember? I'm entitled to do with it whatever I like.'

'I bought the house in your name as a tax break, you and I both know that. Just because the house is in your name certainly didn't give you the right to treat my mother the way you did. Why did you want her out of the house anyway? And don't tell me you were worried about her well-being.'

Suellyn looked at William's face and saw the disgust written there. 'Well if you must know, I wanted it sold because I knew your mother would be better off in a retirement village and because I wanted the money. I'm leaving you, William. I'm fed up.'

William buried his face in his hands, but this didn't stop Suellyn,

'I want a divorce.' Suellyn waited for this piece of information to sink in before she continued. 'And tell me one thing, if you cared so much about your mother, why didn't you bother to look after her yourself, instead of leaving it up to me?'

'Hang on a minute. Before we start casting blame, first things first. What's this about a divorce?'

Suellyn was aware that the owner of the café and the young couple at the corner table were looking at them. Outside, a baby began to cry and Suellyn watched as a young mother stuck a dummy in the baby's mouth to quieten it. 'Keep your voice down for God's sake,' Suellyn hissed, as the waitress placed their orders in front of them. 'Let's be honest with each other for once.' Suellyn continued, quietly but firmly, as she looked into her cup of coffee. 'I know I've made mistakes and I don't really blame you for cheating on me, but with everything that's going on now I've had enough, enough of you, enough of the secrets, enough of the lies.' The froth on the latté had a cocoa powdered heart on the top of it and as she stared at it she wondered if the waitress was playing a cruel joke on her.

'What do you mean, cheated on you? The only mistress I've ever had was my work.'

Suellyn laughed. 'That's a bit rich, isn't it darling? What about Anita, your PA? She even came to your mother's funeral and managed to shed a few tears. And then there was that analyst, what was her name? Peggy, wasn't it? No one knew why she suddenly left. But I did. There was talk, William, and it all got back to me. All those late nights and out of town appointments. Not to mention your overseas' business trips.'

William was surprised by the venom in her voice. 'You're talking rubbish, Suellyn. It was all just drunken, office gossip. You may not know this, but a lot of people I work with are jealous of my lifestyle. I can't believe you didn't trust me enough not to believe the lies they were telling you. I've given you everything and there has never been another woman. Without me you wouldn't have the expensive clothes, jewellery, the flashy car, or a beachside apartment.' William felt his blood pressure rising. He took a bite from his banana bread and a large mouthful of coffee. 'Let's get out of here and go somewhere we can talk privately.'

They both stood. William left a crisp twenty-dollar note on the table and followed Suellyn out of the café, embarrassed by the scene they had caused. As they approached the car park William recognised a familiar buff coloured envelope wedged under the windscreen wipers of his car. 'Shit. What else is going to happen today?' He lifted the windscreen wiper, screwed the parking fine into a tight ball and threw it in the gutter. 'Get in Suellyn.'

She looked at him.

'Now!'

They sat in silence. He gazed momentarily out through the front windscreen and watched as a young woman strapped her baby into a car seat in the car parked in front of him. For the first time in his life, William realised that he was losing control and he had no idea how to rein in his life and bring it back into line. He reversed out of the car space and almost backed into a white delivery truck. He swore. Suellyn was frightened. William had a reputation at work for being hard-bitten and aggressive, but she had never seen that side of him, he had never behaved badly around her and had always been if anything, too reserved, too self-contained.

William was driving too fast, too hard, his cheeks were flushed and pumping. He took one hand off the steering wheel and massaged the knots in the back of his neck with his fingers and Suellyn noticed the deep lines in his forehead. She closed her eyes, held her breath and dug her fingernails into the leather seat.

William made a hard right hand turn into Eden Street and came to an abrupt stop in front of his mother's house. He looked at the 'For Sale' sign in the front yard and then looked over at Suellyn. 'A detonate or renovate' sticker was now plastered across the 'For Sale' sign. How could he have allowed his mother to live like this? If only he'd known, he would have done something to help her. He tried to think back to the last time he'd been to the house. Rose had always visited them at their apartment or else met William at his office in the city. They would often have lunch or morning tea together at the Two Spoons café in George Street. There was a bus stop at the end of Eden Street and it was an easy fifteen minute bus ride to the city. William wondered with all the money she had, why she'd not spent it on herself. She had more than enough money to buy an apartment in the city if she didn't want to go to a retirement village. His mother had spent some of the happiest times of her life in the city when they had lived together in Dora Valentine's boarding house and if he was honest with himself, they were also the happiest times of his life.

Chapter Fifteen

William sat studying me as I added a dash of milk from the bone china milk jug and stirred three full teaspoons of sugar into my cup. As I stirred the tea, the rich, leafy aroma assaulted my senses. The cup was decorated with small, delicate roses and reminded me of a set my mother kept in a glass display cupboard in the dining room of our Ashton Street home.

I slurped the brew noisily and wiped my thin lips with a white napkin. William looked at me expectantly and I felt his mild annoyance as he waited for me to begin. I had something important to tell him, something about his father that I should have told him years ago. I was ashamed of myself and of the lies I had told to protect my reputation; my mind raced and I wondered where I should begin. How was I going to untangle the lies and secrets which had begun the day I walked into Foyle's bookstore and found Douglas Phillips sitting in a dusty corner?

As we sat at a table by the window of the fancy tea shop in George Street, nestled between two high rise office buildings and the wide open space of Martin Place, I stared out onto the street and watched the passersby. I took another sip of the sweet, milky tea, and began my story.

I was born Rose Patricia Evans but changed my family name to Phillips shortly after I met Isabelle Dwyer. I chose the name for no reason other than that I liked the sound of it and I wanted to cut all ties from my previous life. Meeting Isabelle Dwyer was either one of the best or the worst days of my life. There was no doubt in my mind that from the day I first met her, my life changed forever. On reflection, I thought it was for the better, but at times, I imagined that perhaps my life could have taken a more honest course if we had not met.

Edward Baker had a concerned look on his face when he walked through the front door of the narrow shop front on Burke Street on a hot and humid, summer's morning. It was eight am and the dressmaking repairs and alterations business owned by the Rainaldi sisters had just opened its doors for business. Carla and Rosa were out the back making coffee and the deep, rich aroma of Italian ground coffee beans wafted through to the front of the shop where I stood at the counter, preparing for the day's business ahead. His eyes were wide and and he was handsome; in his early forties, he was tall and slim and I was immediately struck by the quality of his suit.

The pair of pinstriped trousers which he pulled out from a paper bag he had tucked under his arm, had a small tear below the knee. He asked if I could mend the trousers as a matter of urgency as he needed them for a special occasion that afternoon. His demeanour relaxed when I said I would attend to it immediately. He turned and smiled at me as he left the shop, and smiled at me again when he returned later that afternoon.

Edward began dropping by the shop on a regular basis after that day to have other clothing mended or altered. I had my suspicions that he bought suits or shirts a size too large just so he could get me to alter them for him. After a few months, with a friendship firmly formed, he had summoned enough courage to ask me out to the Saturday matinee at the local picture theatre. Edward lived with his mother and his maiden aunt and was respectful of women.

I had a great deal of esteem and affection for Edward Baker and enjoyed his attentions and his company, but it was never a great love affair. His mother nagged him constantly to find a wife, to settle down and provide her with grandchildren. She didn't consider me suitable, so he succumbed to her demands and moved on with his life and I moved on with mine. A month later, I discovered I was pregnant with his child.

Mother and father tossed me out of home when they noticed my thickening waist. They guessed my secret long before I had thought of a way of telling them and in the years that followed when I looked back to that time, I consoled myself with the thought that their decision to evict me in such a cruel, heartless manner was done on impulse. We were a Catholic family living in a predominately Catholic neighbourhood and I don't know how my parents explained my sudden departure and what they said to the neighbours when I never returned.

I went to live in Dora Valentine's boarding house, in a working class suburb in the inner city. The rent was within my means as I was always careful with my money right from the start and had a good head for figures. I still had my job with the Italian sisters and the shop was an easy walk from the boarding house, so I settled comfortably into my new life with Dora Valentine.

The boarding house was in a narrow, treeless street. All the houses in the neighbourhood were similar and the shop fronts, like the houses, were narrow, crammed and butted hard up against one another. The front windows were flanked by tall and narrow shutters which were painted a pleasant shade of pea green. The terrace didn't have a verandah and the front door opened directly onto the street. The wash house and the fuel stoves were out the back.

Dora didn't have children, there had been no time in her life for that, or at least, that is what she told me, so it wasn't long before I became Dora's family, and she mine.

Dora Valentine was a practical, hard working woman who was blessed with a heart of gold. She wore her thick dark hair, peppered with grey streaks, in a tight bun at the back of her neck and being a solid woman, her strong arms and straight back, gave the impression that she was someone who was not to be fooled with. Her eyes were bright and blue.

Dora pooled her life savings, converted the terrace into five bed sitters and as luck would have it, my son, Billy and I came to occupy two of the rooms. The main room, the smaller of the two, was a sitting room and the larger which served as our bedroom, was connected to it by a narrow opening. The sitting room was adorned with ornamental ceiling roses and was fourteen feet high. It was painted a soft shade of buttercup yellow, offset by a feature wall covered in wallpaper which was mottled with tiny sprays of white and yellow flowers. The wallpaper ran from the skirting boards to the picture rail and was neatly hung. The rooms were bright and cheerful, especially when the morning sun hit the window panes, throwing in rays of soft, warm light.

As the owner of the boarding house, Dora was popular and well respected in our neighbourhood. Her hands were enormous and she wore a smile as wide as a cricket pitch. Dora Valentine was the only person to know the truth about Billy's father, the handsome soldier who sat silently on my mantelpiece in the sitting room. I had decided to call him Douglas, Douglas Ernest Phillips. Dora often wondered where my lies would lead and what effect it would have on Billy when he eventually discovered the truth, as she knew he would one day. Fortunately, Dora never lived to witness the consequences of my deception and to see that things didn't quite turn out the way I had expected. I should have realised that the lies and deceit I peddled with the aid of Isabelle Dwyer, would one day come back to haunt not only her but Billy and me as well.

I had just had my thirtieth birthday when I walked back through the door of the Rainaldi sisters' dressmaking shop with a baby in my arms and asked for my old job back. They never asked why I left so abruptly without adequate explanation, but it became clear to them when I introduced them to Billy. The sisters were kind-hearted women and assumed that Billy was Edward's son. They cast no judgement on me and as Edward had married and moved away from the area, we never mentioned his name again. With no children of their own, their tears fell and I watched on silently as Carla's nose reddened and the coral lipstick which was applied so generously, smudged against her upper lip as she blew her nose into a delicate lace handkerchief. Rosa, being the more practical of the two, walked over to the till and handed me a five pound note, took Billy from my arms and ordered me to start work immediately.

It was a cloudless autumn day. It was late in the after-noon and the sun was losing the little warmth it had left. But there were still a few hours of sunlight remain-ing when I closed the front door to the shop behind me and took a detour home through a maze of quiet back streets. I knew that Dora wouldn't mind if I was home a little later than usual, she enjoyed looking after Billy on the days that I worked at the shop and a walk in the fresh air would do me the world of good. The street was silent apart from the crunching of dry leaves underfoot. The coppery, golden leaves had begun their annual pilgrimage and fell from the deciduous trees like shrouds, littering the footpaths and front yards of the small inner city blocks. An elderly couple complained to each other that the leaves were a nuisance and I smiled at them as I quickly walked on, eager to avoid the smoky trail of thin smoke which spiraled up from the gutter.

My curiosity suddenly got the better of me and I turned and looked back over my shoulder at the woman wearing a blue checked apron and clutching at a long handled straw broom. She was sweeping bright piles of leaves into tidy mounds as her male companion sat quietly on his haunches, rocking backwards and forwards, humming to himself as he tendered the smoldering flames. The couple didn't look at each other but their connection was plain to see, even to a stranger's eyes.

The route I had chosen was not my usual way home and I soon became disoriented as I passed through a number of streets and dirty, rubbish filled back lanes. A group of school boys chasing a football and dressed in ill-fitting grey uniforms, jostled me as I turned the corner into Cunningham Street.

The street was one-way and I tripped on an empty beer bottle as I stepped off the footpath into the deep sandstone gutter to cross to the other side of the street. I swore silently to myself as I looked down at the bottle's amber neck poking out from a crumpled, paper bag. I clutched my handbag in one hand and straightened my stockings with the other; suddenly feeling foolish, I looked around to see if anyone had seen me stumble. I kicked the bottle to one side, annoyed by the carelessness of a thoughtless drunk.

I regained my composure, raised my nose to the air and sniffed at the singed, burnt smell of freshly ironed shirts as it wafted and snaked its way towards me. It was a familiar scent, a scent which strangely comforted me and was a homely reminder of what I once had.

A solidly built woman stood on the top of a set of worn sandstone steps in a doorway. Her hands were placed firmly on her hips as if she was about to scold. I expected her to ask if I had hurt myself and wondered why she looked at me in the manner in which she did. Perhaps she was not looking at me at all, but simply taking time to catch her breath, and to contemplate the task which lay ahead.

Muscled, nut-brown arms poked out from her sleeveless shift and her limp hair was tied back with a red ribbon. When she noticed me looking at her, she turned away and returned to her work. With her body slumped over a large pile of clothes, she began to sort and empty drawstring bags. The contents spewed out onto the chessboard linoleum floor and I wondered if customers ever complained of lost articles of clothing.

A hand painted sign on the glass window caught my eye. 'Lucky's Laundromat, Washes Whites Whiter With Rinso' was painted in large, bold letters. I found myself smiling at the alliteration and wondered if Lucky was a person's name or was a comment on the establishment's prosperity. I walked on and left the comforting smells of domesticity behind me.

The street veered sharply to the right and disappeared around a bend. I followed it on, past a disused clothing factory which was boarded up with a large 'For Sale' sign affixed to the front of the building. I stopped in the middle of the footpath. The way ahead was blocked by a large blackboard sign.

'Foyle's Bookstore-Books Bought and Sold' was written carefully in white chalk on the board. There were flourishes in the writing and it was obvious that the scribe had taken great care with it. The book store reminded me of Dickens' Old Curiosity Shop and I found myself strangely drawn to it, wondering what I would find behind its freshly painted door. I turned the brass knob and pushed firmly against it. A bell sounded above my head as I entered and a red headed young man dressed in a suit, and a middle aged woman wearing a pale complexion and bright red lips looked up from their books. An elderly man with a toothbrush moustache sat at the sales counter and nodded, the young man frowned, the woman smiled a wide smile and brushed away a strand of hair which had fallen across her cheek. The trio, having accepted my presence, returned to their books. The disruption I had caused, having been forgiven.

The bookstore was dimly lit and it took a moment for my eyes to adjust to the room after the hazy, autumn sunlight outside. 'Foyle's on Cunningham' was a small, airless bookstore but I felt safe within its walls. The smell of leather, ink and dusty books was strangely comforting and it was an ideal place to hide away from the world, if only for a short time on an autumn afternoon. I was quietly reassured by the store's cosy silence and quickly decided on my purchases – a picture book for Billy and a romance novel for Dora. The clip to my purse clicked sharply between my thumb and forefinger as I checked to see if I had enough money for my purchases. A crumpled one pound note poked out from where I usually kept my loose coins and I sighed, relieved at the thought of money in my purse.

My eyes wandered over the books. They were crammed into the ceiling high book shelves and fell at odd angles against each other, like rugby players in a packed scrum and I found myself softly touching their spines, studying their titles and the authors to see if, like old friends, I recognised any of them.

Large piles of books and magazines sat precariously on the timber floor and despite their lack of order, I was impressed by their quality. Behind a row of shelves, I found a wicker basket filled with a collection of old photographs. My father had been a keen amateur photographer after he returned from The War. A large walk-in cupboard under the back stairs of our Ashton Street home had been transformed into a small darkroom and if he was in an agreeable mood and had not been drinking, he would allow me to slide the photo paper into the developer tray and slosh it around until an image magically appeared.

With his Leica camera slung over his shoulder, on most Sundays after Church, father took the 362 bus into town. It was unusual for him to return before early evening and when he finally did arrive home, he disappeared into the cupboard under the stairs and reappeared only when Mother called him for tea.

The photos he took were an exposé of people and their lives, all kinds of people and all kinds of lives. A nervous shudder brought me back to the present as I looked again towards the wicker basket, strangely drawn to its contents by memories from the past.

A cardboard box overflowing with Captain Marvel comics sat next to the basket beneath a timber hatstand. A colourful sombrero sat on top of the hatstand and a black embroidered jacket was draped over one of the polished, brass hooks. A souvenir from someone's travels, I thought, or perhaps it was going to be part of a display on Spanish culture. Books on cacti and Spanish architecture were littered on the dark timbered sales counter and the elderly man, whom I presumed was the owner, sat perched on a stool. He was flicking through the pages of a book and looked irritated as if he was in search of some important fact which he was unable to locate. His steel rimmed glasses slipped and his eyes squinted as he attempted to push them back onto the bridge of his nose. He looked up at me from behind his book and studied me for a moment before he smiled. His eyes darted from me to the hatstand and back again. He moved the book to one side. 'Do you know anything about Spain?'

I was about to answer, but he didn't wait for my reply.

'I'm putting together a display, it's a fascinating country. My nephew was there in thirty-eight, during the Civil war. After hearing about his experiences, I became obsessed, such a passionate people, such an interesting country.' He placed his hand gently on the pile of books in front of him and shook his head. 'Might as well read all I can because I doubt I'll ever get there now, too old,' he said, as he scratched the grey whiskers on his chin. 'Let me know if you need any help,' he said almost as an afterthought.

I returned my thoughts and my attention to the wicker basket and the collection of old photos. I sorted through one familiar inner city street scene after another and then a number of construction photos of the Sydney Harbour Bridge. I put them all to one side and dug further into the basket and then I came across a photo of a soldier dressed in an Australian Army uniform. I held the photo in my hands. It was a professional portrait and the size was such that it allowed me to distinguish his features clearly. I was intrigued. What act had he been guilty of that would have him abandoned in such a way? Perhaps he had a falling out with his wife or lover. I examined the photo closely and held it up to the light filtering through the glass shop front. He was about my age and had an innocent look about him, which I found attractive. He looked vulnerable even though he was dressed in a soldier's uniform and, I imagined as I stared into his eyes, that I may have seen him before – passed him in a busy street or caught a glimpse of him as we boarded a train to a shared destination. His dark, wavy hair was neatly combed and parted in the middle, a lopsided grin revealed a perfect set of teeth. I liked that. I decided to take him home.

Billy spent his childhood and part of his adult life thinking his father was a hero. I gleaned all the information I needed from past newspapers I found at the library, studied them and recorded the details of a World War II battle in Europe in a small yellow spiral notebook I kept in the top drawer of my bedside table. By doing this, I invented a plausible time line for Douglas's life, a fabrication based on part truths and my own imaginings of the man I dreamt could have been the father of my son, a father he would never know. I carefully placed the photo in a frame and put it on the timber mantelpiece *above the small coke fireplace in the sitting room and called him Douglas, Douglas Ernest Phillips. It wasn't long before I began to believe that he really was my husband and as time passed, I was surprised that Billy never asked about his father. He didn't seem to notice that he bore no physical resemblance to the soldier whose photo sat next to the small, blue porcelain dinner bell on the mantelpiece. Billy told me later that as a child, he had felt his father's eyes follow him around the sitting room, passing quiet judgement on him. He ignored the soldier on the mantelpiece and attached little significance to the man I chose to be his father. I often wondered who he was, the soldier who I picked up from the bookstore that day and wove into the threads of my life.*

As the years moved on, so did my Billy. He was no longer Billy, but William and I was to refer to him as such, especially in company.

He occasionally invited me to afternoon tea at our favourite tea shop in the city, not far from where he worked. As we sat drinking our tea in ivory coloured porcelain teacups with tiny pink roses around the rim and eating fluffy scones, covered in sticky jam and luscious cream, he said he wanted to do something for me. I didn't pay much attention at the time - I couldn't have known what he was thinking.

It was just after Billy married Suellyn that he bought the house in Eden Street. I was surprised when he and Suellyn picked me up in his fancy car one morning and we drove out of the city, away from the boarding house to the leafy suburb. He pulled up outside the house and I sat there for some time looking at the house and the street wondering how I could live here, a place that seemed to me to be so far away from the life I led in the city.

The three of us, Suellyn, Billy and I, stepped out of the car, closed the doors behind us and walked across the grass nature strip, through the timber gate and up to the front door. Whenever I looked at the front door from that day on, I always thought of the day I moved to Eden Street. I couldn't believe that anyone could be so kind, not even my own son. A wonderful gift to someone who never really expected anything from anybody. Tears welled in my eyes and I remember that I had to wipe them away so I wouldn't look like the silly woman that I was.

I stood in the doorway and hugged Billy for a long time, so long that I know he was embarrassed. He cleared his throat, moved my arms away gently and led me through the house to the kitchen. He apologised to me that the house was run-down and needed work done to it. Suellyn said she would see to all of that, but she never did. I suppose she never found the time.

People didn't want to live in the city anymore. There was a real push, especially in the fifties, for families to find a block of land and build a house somewhere away from the dirt and the noise, out in the suburbs somewhere. Living in the inner city was not regarded as a respectable place to live. It had the reputation of being a slum. Most of my friends had already moved of course, there was more money about but I never did understand why people wanted to leave. The city was alive with interesting smells, it was vibrant, full of noise from the traffic and people going about their daily lives.

I was sad to leave the boarding house at first, but Billy insisted, especially as Dora had recently died and the boarding house was on the market, but I soon settled into my new life. I was lucky with my neighbours, especially, Kevin Taggart and Edi and Rhoda Blake.

Kevin Taggert was always a good neighbour to me and I never did say a proper thank you to him. I was embarrassed by his kindness and embarrassed by the circumstances in which I had found myself. He kept much to himself and I kept to myself. A couple of hermits the both of us. Kevin had his painting and I had my crosswords and, of course, I had Astrid.

Astrid was an extremely intelligent cat with a rather unique voice. She was my only true friend, apart from Max Gray. She kept me warm at nights, especially after it turned cold and the electricity had been disconnected. I liked her chatting away to me in her deep, loud voice, more like a dog than a cat. I loved her playfulness and affectionate nature and she was always climbing onto my kitchen table, showing off her long slender legs. Often when she was looking for attention from me she would climb onto my bony shoulders and look into my wrinkly old face with her blue, almond shaped eyes. Suellyn will have her put to sleep after I'm gone. She didn't care much for cats.

A new neighbour moved in, next to Kevin. She looked friendly with her neat haircut, and designer clothing and I thought she was going to speak to me on the day I died, when I was on my way to the shops and she was returning home. It was a shame that she didn't have the time to stop and say, 'Hello.'

Chapter Sixteen

Tommy looked down the row of backlit buzzers affixed to the facade of the Panorama Apartments and pressed the intercom button marked 16. He checked his watch; he didn't realise it was so late. While he waited for an answer, he wiped away a wet drip from his nose with the back of his hand. Waves crashed onto the beach and filled the night air with a fine mist. He ran his tongue over his lips and tasted the salt.

'Hello?' Suellyn wasn't expecting anyone, especially at this time of night.

'Sues, it's me, Tommy.' He spoke into the intercom slowly and clearly, not knowing whether he could be heard. He ran his hand over his chin, it felt like sandpaper and he realised that he'd forgotten to shave.

'Tommy, what are you doing here?' she whispered. 'William's home, you should have phoned first.'

'I don't care. We need to talk. I need to talk to both of you. William needs to know the truth.'

'Okay then, come on up.' Suellyn pressed the

security door release button and waited for a moment before she asked, 'Are you in?'

Tommy didn't answer, but Suellyn heard the distinctive click of the door as the lock released and the entrance door shut. She opened the door to the apartment before Tommy had a chance to knock. She flinched at the sight of him as his body framed the doorway. His hands were in the pockets of a pair of black jeans and the bomber jacket he was wearing gave him a youthful appearance. His cheeks were flushed from the cold, his hair unruly, ruffled by the wind. As he gazed into Suellyn's eyes, he tilted his head to one side, sheepishly, as if he expected her to suddenly take him in her arms and kiss him. When he realised that this wasn't going to happen he didn't wait for her to invite him in. He shot her a smile, kissed her hard on the lips anyway, nudged past her and walked down the hallway and into the lounge-room. Tommy knew the apartment like the back of his hand and looked about for William.

'Hello,' William said. He was holding an opened bottle of red wine in one hand and two wine glasses in the other. William was annoyed, but not surprised by the sight of him. He was hoping to spend a quiet evening alone with Suellyn to find out if there was anything left in their marriage worth saving and to find out more about Tommy Dwyer. Now he would have a chance to find out about Tommy without having to ask his wife. 'We met at the funeral,' William said, as a statement of fact. He put down the wine glasses and offered his hand. Tommy grabbed it firmly.

'Have a seat. Would you like a glass?' He raised

the bottle. 'Suellyn and I were just about to have one.' William looked at Suellyn. She was standing in the middle of the lounge room, looking awkward, guilt written on her face like tarnished silver waiting to be polished. They had both calmed down after the outburst earlier in the day but William knew Suellyn well enough to know that he had to keep her calm if he wanted to get some answers from her.

'Thanks, I could do with a glass of vino,' Tommy said. 'It's blowing a gale outside.'

Suellyn looked at Tommy and noticed the smug look on his face and the cockiness in his manner. William knew from years of legal negotiations that Tommy Dwyer looked as if he knew he was holding all the aces. His eyes were bright, his lips moist. The expression splashed across Tommy's face was one that Suellyn had never seen before. He turned away from her, accepted a glass of wine from William and made himself comfortable on the leather lounge. Suellyn draped a pale blue pashmina around her shoulders and sat opposite him on the ottoman and looked at the two men, wondering who would speak first.

It was William who broke the awkward silence. 'Suellyn tells me you live up the coast and that you are a friend of Kerry Dawson.'

Tommy nodded and took a large mouthful of wine. Tommy wasn't here for small talk and he had never heard of a Kerry Dawson. A fabrication no doubt thought up by Suellyn to explain how she knew him. 'William,' he paused for a moment to gather his thoughts, 'at the funeral, I said that your mother and I went way back.'

'Yes, I remember you saying something like that.' William leant over and topped up Tommy's glass trying to make light of the situation they had all found themselves in. William had a gut feeling after their meeting at Rose's funeral that Tommy Dwyer was going to turn up again one day and here he was. He didn't like this cocky fellow sitting across from him in his apartment, drinking his expensive wine and looking at his wife in a way which suggested that they were more than just friends. William decided to get in first before Tommy had a chance to take control of the conversation. 'Before you say anything Tommy, I know from Rose's will that you're probably my half-brother. Some sordid story no doubt. So, let's cut to the chase, which half are you?'

'William,' Tommy hesitated for a moment, then looked him square in the eye.

'Rose is... well, I'm sorry to be the one to tell you, but Rose wasn't your birth mother. We're half brothers, same mother but different fathers.'

William's body straightened as if it had just turned to stone. For the first time in his life, he didn't know how to respond. The answer wasn't the answer he'd been expecting. William knew he had just broken the first rule of cross examination, never ask a question to which you don't already know the answer. He placed his glass of wine down carefully on the coffee table, not trusting himself not to spill it, and sat down on the lounge chair opposite Tommy. He gave him a puzzled look, a please explain kind of look.

'What do you mean Rose wasn't my mother? Of course she was.' William's dark eyes narrowed and darted towards Suellyn. 'Tell me you don't know any-thing about this.'

Suellyn looked down at her hands and fiddled with her wedding band. By not answering he knew she knew.

William's heart pounded painfully through his chest as if Suellyn held it in her hands and was squeez-ing it, squeezing it hard, hard enough that it felt as if it was about to explode and break through his chest.

Suellyn pouted her lips as a small child does who was not used to not getting her own way. She put her head in her hands and began to sob. Tommy drained the remaining drops of his wine and placed his glass on the coffee table next to William's.

'Somebody, tell me what's going on,' William demanded.

'As I said, you're my half-brother and Rose wasn't your birth mother. I don't really know what else to tell you or what it is you want to know,' Tommy said goading William in a toneless, flat voice.

William walked out onto the terrace and gulped the fresh air greedily, as if it were a glass of iced water. He moved to the edge of the balcony and grabbed the top of the railing. With his feet spread wide to balance himself, his eyes blinked and watered with the force of the wind. It was gusting at least thirty knots and William stood looking out to sea like a ship's captain standing at the prow of his doomed ship, knowing what was to come, waiting for the next giant wave to strike and engulf him. His self-confidence had been stripped away, he felt raw and naked, it was as if the person he thought he was, no longer existed. The ocean was wild tonight. The coal black waves tumbled over each other in the shallows with a roar; piggy backing each other like survivors of a ship wreck in a scramble to make it to shore. He took another deep breath, this time filling every inch of his lungs with the smell and power of the ocean, trying to take in the information, absorbing it, casting it about in his mind, and wondering what he would do with it. The sky was full with growling dark clouds, thunder was stalking in the distance, the ocean was ripping itself apart. William wiped his eyes and tugged at his hair. He turned around slowly and walked back inside to face the truth and to face Tommy Dwyer.

He stood looking at his half-brother for a moment before he spoke. 'There's more to all of this. You aren't telling me everything, so let's start with where have you been all my life? It was bad enough being lied to by my mother about the identity of my father. And by the way, I still don't know the answer to that question. I wanted nothing more to do with her and never forgave her for leading me on like that, encouraging me to believe that a photo of some soldier she found in a dusty second hand bookshop could be a substitute for a father. Making me think for all those years that he was some great war hero and that he died before I was born. What a joke.' William paced around the room. 'If only she'd been honest with me and for that matter, honest with herself right from the beginning. She was such a stupid woman.'

Tommy looked down at his feet attempting to suppress the pleasure he was experiencing from William's outburst.

'Enough of talking about Rose, I'm on a roll here. Have I got this right? My mother was not my mother, my father was not my father, but you are my half-brother and can I also assume that you are having an affair with my wife?' William was pacing backwards and forwards now, like some caged, wild animal, rubbing the back of his neck with his head bowed, his fists clenched. 'Suellyn, did you know that lover boy here was my brother when you started cheating on me?'

'Of course I didn't. Tommy and I met at a bar in town and we just sort of clicked. It was as simple as that, a chance meeting. Besides, our marriage was already over in my mind.'

Suellyn reminded William of a pathetic clown, her tears had caused her mascara to bleed, thick, black tracks ran down her cheeks, her lipstick was half eaten away and her hair was disheveled. She blew her nose loudly into a tissue and when she had finished, she stuffed the crumpled square into the pocket of her jeans.

Suellyn crossed her arms firmly against her chest. She had finished with the hysterics, now she was just mad. 'I'm sick to death of all the lies and secrets! I don't need any of this.'

William drank from his glass and was about to take another mouthful, but decided against it. He knew he had to remain sober. He was already too upset and perhaps already a little too drunk. He knew he needed a clear head so he could deal with this. He slammed the glass down on the coffee table for effect as much as anything else and was not upset that the contents spilled over the pile of Vogue magazines he knew that Suellyn had not yet read. 'You're sick of the secrets! Christ, Suellyn, after everything that's been dumped on me tonight, you're going on about secrets?' William's mind was racing but his legal instinct was starting to kick in. He turned from Suellyn to Tommy. He was trying to control his desire to grab him by the throat, drag him out onto the terrace and throw him over the railing onto the street below. 'Okay, one thing at a time,' William said coolly. 'Would you mind telling me who my mother and father are, Tommy, or at least who they were?'

There was a pause. Tommy looked around the room before he began. 'My mother, Isabelle Dwyer,' Tommy shifted in his seat. 'I mean our mother, died about six months ago. When I was going through her garage to clean out the rubbish she had accumulated over the years, I found a couple of cardboard boxes hidden behind a row of shelves. She'd probably forgotten that they were even there. I didn't bother to look through them at the time. I was a bit emotional, understandably so. I just packed them up and took them back to my house along with a few other things that had sentimental value. I'd forgotten all about the boxes until recently when I was going through my wardrobe sorting out all my junk for a garage sale I was planning to have. When I found the boxes next to my golf clubs, I went through them more for curiosity sake than anything else and discovered a letter from my mother to Rose Phillips. It confirmed what I already knew about the circumstances surrounding your birth. I also found other letters to Rose and I must tell you, at the time, I found the whole thing quite shocking. My pious mother. Anyway, I digress.

147

To cover up the mess she'd found herself in, she told my father she wanted to travel abroad for six months to visit her parents in England. My father indulged her, as he so often did. I don't know whether he ever expected anything at the time but he let her go anyway. I know he found out some years later because before he died he told me the whole story.'

William was not aware that his mouth was open. He stared at Tommy. 'But what's all this got to do with Rose? Where does she fit into all of this?' William asked incredulously.

'That's the next part of the story. It gets worse I'm afraid,' Tommy said as he scratched the side of his forehead. 'But before I tell you, can I have another drink, something a little stronger this time?'

William grabbed the whisky bottle and a clean glass from the sideboard. 'Well?' he said as he handed Tommy the glass. 'Get on with it, we haven't got all night.'

Tommy took a swig and looked into the glass, then his eyes lifted and he looked back at William. He was enjoying watching William squirm. 'Before Isabelle left for England, she went to the Northside Hospital for a check up. I suppose she wanted to make sure that the pregnancy was still viable. You know, to make sure that she was still pregnant. Imagine if she had gone to all the trouble of travelling to England for nothing. Her plan was to have the baby in London, adopt it out and return home as if nothing had happened. Very calculating our mother, don't you think William?'

William didn't say a word.

When Tommy realised William wasn't going to

say anything, he continued. 'Well this is where Rose comes into the picture. Rose Evans just happened to be sitting next to mother in the waiting room. Rose had lost her baby, an early term miscarriage apparently. Her parents had already kicked her out of home and the father had done a runner. Isabelle being the sort of person who could see an opportunity when there was one, took advantage of the situation and came up with a plan which would benefit them both.

Isabelle and Rose travelled to London on the *SS Arcadia*. She had it planned well. She paid for Rose's passage on what you call a slow boat to London and arrived at Tilbury Dock where she was met by her cousin, Hetti Blakehurst. She didn't tell her parents she was in the country, all very hush, hush.' Tommy took another mouthful of whisky and continued. 'It was all organised, Rose would be recorded on the birth certificate as the birth mother and Douglas Phillips as the father, a fictitious name Rose had thought up. Isabelle had already organized a midwife who was open to a bribe or baby bonus as Isabelle called it and her cousin Hetti worked at the Registry of Births, Deaths and Marriages so falsifying the records was straightforward. Isabelle gave birth to you three months after arriving on English soil and then just handed you over to Rose. With no family to speak of, Rose was more than happy to go ahead with the arrangement if it meant that she would have the baby she longed for. Simple, really. Apparently, nobody asked any questions, either here, or in England. Rose was your mother, a mysterious man called Douglas Phillips was your father and you were their son. Isabelle stuck to her side of the bargain and supported you and Rose financially until you left school. After going through her bank accounts it looks like she paid for some of your university fees as well.'

'But why did Isabelle go to all the trouble of taking Rose with her. Why not simply adopt me out and then return home?' William asked.

'Isabelle realised that she couldn't go through the whole business on her own. She needed Rose for support and companionship. She knew Rose would look after her. After all, you have to remember Rose was a stakeholder in all of this. And as far as adoption, I can only assume that she didn't want her name to be associated with any official record of your birth. Isabelle and Rose had a pact based on guilt and loss, but in the end they both won out. Isabelle's respectability remained intact and Rose had the baby she thought she had lost forever. Rose sent photos of you, but I don't think Isabelle was that interested or maybe she just wanted to forget the whole thing. As far as she was concerned, she had only one son and that son was me, the one and only, Tommy Seymour Dwyer.'

They sat in silence.

William didn't know what to say. Words failed him as he stormed out of the apartment and left Suellyn and Tommy sitting together in the lounge-room. Neither of them knew where to look or what to do.

'You should have told me Tommy, you should have told me from the beginning that William was your brother. I would never have got involved with you if I'd known. What am I supposed to do now?'

'You'll have to work it out for yourself Suellyn. I'm

fed up with all this drama. At least the truth's out now.' Tommy pulled himself up from the lounge and walked towards the door. He was a little unsteady on his feet, he didn't know whether it was from the alcohol or from all the emotion that had been floating around the apartment. He turned and looked at Suellyn sitting on the ottoman clutching the glass of whisky in her hand, her hair was loose. 'Don't worry Suellyn, don't get up on my account, I'll see myself out. I'm staying at *The Barclay Hotel* in town if you want to talk.'

Suellyn stared after him as the door closed behind him.

Chapter Seventeen

Suellyn parked her Porsche outside the house in Eden Street, and walked up the steps, across the verandah to the front door and fumbled with her keys before scraping them against the lock. The house had been shut up since the day Rose died and the air smelt like rotting stone fruit and sweaty socks. Suellyn stood still and listened. The house was drowning in silence, all was quiet apart from the slow ticking of the kitchen clock.

She put her handbag down on the lounge and prowled around the house, visiting each room wondering where an old woman would hide something she considered important. She walked into the kitchen and rummaged through the dresser drawers and the cupboards where Rose had kept her pots and pans. She picked up the tea caddy, unscrewed the lid and looked inside. 'It's got to be here somewhere,' she said as she made her way into Rose's bedroom. She'd looked in the bedroom before, when Rose had been preoccupied with her tea making, but this time she looked with different eyes. She tried to think where Rose would have hidden Isabelle's letter.

The room was just as her mother-in-law had left it. Her lace-up shoes and slippers sat side-by-side on the floor next to her bed. As she sat down on the saggy mattress, Suellyn looked at the framed photo on the bedside table. She fingered it gently before picking it up. William had been such a handsome baby. She studied the black and white photo carefully before she pulled back the metal spikes that held the glass and the photo in the frame, and prodded her fingernail in between the cardboard and the photo. A sheet of writing paper fell from the frame into her lap. She smiled and her shoulders suddenly straightened, her eyes were wide like saucers. She unfolded the sheet of paper. This was what she had been looking for. It was here all the time. The dust from the faded pink chenille bedspread made her sneeze and she wiped her nose with the back of her hand. The letter was dated three weeks before Isabelle Dwyer had committed suicide. It was apparent from the letter, that Tommy's mother and Rose had a friendship spanning decades which had been clouded in secrecy, deceit and lies.

'What have you found Suellyn?' William stood in the doorway of Rose's bedroom. His voice was accusing.

'Nothing. Just a baby photo of you.' Suellyn slipped the crumpled letter into the pocket of her coat.

William walked towards the bed and looked at the photo and the frame lying next to Suellyn. She stood up from the bed.

Suellyn, what's going on?' he said in a raised voice. 'What are you doing here?'

'Nothing,' she replied.

'Don't lie to me.' He slapped her across the face with his open hand and Suellyn dropped to the floor. William slumped down beside her. Their backs dug into the steel bed frame and Suellyn's cheek was smarting. Shocked, she held her hand against her face, tears welling in her eyes.

William looked at his wife through rolling tears. 'Suellyn, I'm sorry, forgive me. I didn't mean to...' his voice quivered. 'I just don't know what's going on any-more. The woman who I thought was my mother is dead, my birth mother died without me even knowing her, you want a divorce, real estate agents are hanging around like vultures and this guy Dwyer appears from out of the blue claiming to be my brother, it's just all too much. It's all so unreal, it's like I'm playing out some character in a cheap thriller. I know I should've forgiven my mother, I'm sorry for that now.' William shook his head and looked down at his legs 'splayed out in front of him. 'If I'd only listened to her when she tried to tell me about the business with my father all those years ago. I just got up and walked out of the café. I should have let her explain. She wanted to tell me, but like a fool, I wouldn't listen.'

Suellyn looked at William. She didn't know what to think or to say. She'd never seen him cry before.

'You know I never cheated on you Suellyn, hon-estly, despite what you think. All the times I said I was working, I really was. How do you think I got to be a where I am at Stockland Lewis, it wasn't by playing around that's for sure.'

William pulled out a handkerchief from his trouser pocket and blew his nose. Suellyn looked at William and realised they had both made a lot of mistakes.

Chapter Eighteen

Kevin placed his paintbrush behind his ear and pulled out the phone from the sagging pocket of his tracksuit pants. When he answered, he tried to disguise his annoyance at being rung so late at night.

'Hello Kevin, I'm sorry to disturb you at this late hour, but I didn't know who else to call,' Rhoda Blake apologised to him in a frail, frightened voice.

'What's the matter Miss Blake, has something happened to Edi?' Kevin was genuinely concerned; he could tell from the tone in Rhoda's voice that she was upset.

'No. It's not Edi, she's fine. But I think there's someone outside the house. Edi said she heard a noise and thought she saw a prowler outside her bedroom window. We're both a bit nervous, especially after what happened to poor Rose. Some of the neighbours have been saying that she was murdered.'

'That's rubbish and you know it. I'll be right over to sort things out. Now don't you go worrying yourself about anything.' Kevin put his paintbrush in a jar of water and stared at the canvas in front of him. 'It's probably just a possum or a tomcat prowling around,' Kevin reassured her.

'You're probably right, but please can you hurry, Kevin? Edi is so upset. I haven't seen her this upset since Rose's funeral.'

Kevin hung up the phone and wrapped his dressing gown tightly around his bulging waistline and knotted the cord. He wondered if he should change into something more suitable but Rhoda had sounded distraught and was insistent that he come immediately.

It was ten-fifteen and the night air was chilly. The automatic sensor light lit up as Kevin sat down on the back steps and pulled on his muddy, knee-high black rubber boots and a pair of woollen gloves. He grabbed a yellow Dolphin torch from his tool box, turned it on and hurried across the street. Eden Street was deathly quiet but it wasn't unusual for it to be so quiet at this time of night. The street was filled with elderly residents and the only disturbance was the occasional screech from fruit bats as they flew overhead on their way to the clump of fig trees in the park across the river.

Kevin put on a concerned neighbour face and knocked at the front door. The outside coach light lit up almost immediately. The door opened and Kevin realised that Edi and Rhoda had been waiting for him behind the door, both anxious and afraid.

'Kevin, it's you. Thank goodness you're here. We've been so worried.'

'No need to worry, I'm sure it's nothing, probably just a couple of ring-tail possums. I've brought a torch with me. I'll go and have a good look around the backyard.'

Rhoda was glad that she had such a dependable neighbour in Kevin Taggart. Someone she could trust and rely on. Rhoda locked the door as Kevin walked down the front steps. He made his way around to the side of the house and as he skirted the perimeter of the property he shone his torch up and down the walls of the house and checked the boughs of the gum trees next to the neighbours' fences. After spending almost five minutes walking around the backyard, Kevin was convinced that everything was in order. As he switched off the torch and walked around to the front of the house he brushed against a spider's web draped between two bushes. He ran his fingers over his face and through his hair, frantically trying to remove the fine, sticky web. Taking two steps at a time, he sprinted up the front steps and knocked twice on the door which was the prearranged signal.

Rhoda opened the door.

'Nothing to worry about, everything appears to be in order.'

I'm so grateful, Kevin. It's such a comfort knowing that you're just across the street at times like this.' Rhoda had regained her composure, the fear she had displayed earlier had disappeared completely. She asked Kevin to join her and Edi in a nightcap – to settle everyone's nerves. Kevin removed his rubber boots and left them on the verandah by the front door. He padded behind Rhoda in his bare feet across the timber floorboards down the hallway and into the lounge-room.

The television was blaring.

'Turn the television down Edi, we have a visitor.'

Kevin sat down on one of the chairs next to the lounge, stretched out his legs and wriggled his toes in front of the gas heater. It was on high and the room was hot and stuffy. 'I reckon it was probably just a possum. You know what the cheeky devils are like,' Kevin said, as Rhoda poured him a sherry. Edi looked baffled. She wondered what the barefooted man dressed in his dressing gown was doing at this time of night sitting in their lounge-room, sipping their sherry.

The two sisters sat side by side on the lounge. Both were in their sleepwear and Kevin averted his eyes when he noticed Edi's embarrassment. He pulled the gold dressing gown cord tighter around his waist. The dressing gown was at least fifteen years old and was fashioned from a coarse, saddle brown material. It smelt of mothballs and a fine mustard coloured check ran through the pattern. A strand of oily hair fell into his eyes. He ran his fingers over his skull and dragged the stray hair back to where it belonged with one hand and drained the contents of a delicate crystal sherry glass with the other. After ten minutes of idle chat and two more glasses of sherry, Kevin knew it was time he left. He walked over to the gas heater.

'They don't make gas heaters like this anymore,' he said to Rhoda. Kevin adjusted the control on the top of the heater and placed his woollen gloved hands into the pockets of his dressing gown. 'Well, goodnight ladies. Sleep tight, don't let the bed bugs bite. You don't need to worry about anything.'

Rhoda stood up, took another mouthful of

sherry. She was unsteady on her feet and swayed in a zig zag fashion up the hall to the front door. She placed a trembling hand on Kevin's arm.

'Thank you so much Kevin,' Rhoda slurred. 'You are such a fine gentleman and you are very, very kind. It's a comfort to know that we have such a wonderful, caring neighbour. We don't have anyone else we can call on you know, you're our knight in shining armour.'

Kevin wondered if she was serious. 'Knight in shining armour?' he laughed, gave a quick backwards wave over his shoulder, walked down the front steps and out through the front gate.

'Rhoda Blake, I hope you and Edi have changed your wills like you said you would, you know I'm counting on you,' he spoke to himself in a hushed tone as he crossed the street but Rhoda had already closed the front door. She walked back into the lounge-room and joined Edi on the lounge and poured each of them another large sherry. She took a sip from the crystal glass and took her sister's hand in hers. Edi had the remote control in her other hand and turned up the volume. The late movie had just begun.

The first things Ashleigh noticed as she turned into Eden Street, were the red and blue lights flashing outside the Blake house which was cordoned off with fluttering police tape. Three ambulances and two police trucks were parked outside. It was always a bad omen when more than one ambulance was called to a scene Ashleigh thought as she parked the Landcruiser at the top of her driveway. She dragged the handbrake on and grabbed her handbag from the floor in front of the passenger seat. She jumped down from her vehicle leaving the driver's door wide open and pulled her ID from her handbag. She flashed it at the police officer who was walking towards her. He waved her on. White suited men and women were everywhere. A young female police officer held the crime scene tape up for her as she ducked underneath.

'What's happening here?' Ashleigh asked.

'A couple of old ladies dead in the lounge-room. The TV's still running, all the lights are on and there's a strong smell of gas. The neighbour across the road made the call to 000 after he went to check on them when he noticed the lounge room lights were still on after midnight.'

'Oh God.' Ashleigh ran up the concrete path towards the front steps of the house.

'Ashleigh?'

She recognised Kevin Taggart's voice. What did he want? She stopped in the doorway under the verandah's coach light and looked back over her shoulder at her neighbour. He was standing under the street light in front of his house wearing a dressing gown, his hair was standing on end as if he had been woken from a deep sleep. Looking as if he was enjoying the show he crossed the street and stood in the gutter, behind the crime scene tape.

'Isn't it terrible? Poor Edith and Rhoda,' he called out to her. 'What a terrible way to die, an awful accident. Must have been Edi, you know what she was like.'

Ashleigh stared at Kevin and didn't say a word. His flabby chest was exposed to the night air and a pair of striped pyjama pants was visible beneath his dressing gown. A gold cord hung from his hips. He was wearing knee-high rubber gardening boots which Ashleigh thought odd. She turned away from him and entered the house. Edi and Rhoda were slumped up against each other on the lounge. Edi was dressed in a soft pink, flannelette nightdress buttoned to her throat. A pink ribbon was neatly tied in a bow on her chest and she was wearing matching satin slippers. Her hair was secured tightly in plastic rollers. Rhoda was wearing what looked to be a pair of designer pyjamas. She was barefooted and a pair of slippers was on the floor next to the gas heater. They both looked so peaceful, so ordinary, as if they had fallen asleep together watching a late movie in front of the television set.

'Somebody turn that TV off for Christ's sake,' Rimis said as he approached Ashleigh. 'What's going on here Ashleigh? This is some neighbourhood you've moved into. Two more neighbours dead. What is it with the old ladies around here?'

Ashleigh was only half listening to Nick Rimis. She had her own theory. 'Maybe they knew the perp. They were both trusting, they would have opened the door to anyone, especially if the intruder had a good excuse and they knew them.'

'Ash, we aren't ruling out some sort of suicide pact here or perhaps what our good friend Kevin has suggested, dementia and gas heaters. Not a good combination in anyone's books.'

'I just can't believe it. They wouldn't do anything like that. Rhoda had her wits about her, she always kept a close eye on Edi. They were devoted to each other; there was no reason for them to take their own lives.'

'I'll walk you home; you look like you could do with a drink.' Rimis placed his hand on her back and guided her out of the lounge-room, through the front door and across the street to where Kevin Taggart was standing under the street light in front of his house. Ashleigh noticed all the lights in the houses in the street were on and the elderly residents were all standing around in their dressing gowns.

Rimis and Ashleigh passed Kevin as he stood at the top of his driveway. Kevin looked like he was about to say something but decided against it when he saw the look on DS Rimis's face.

'I'll speak to you later, Kevin. Put the jug on.'

Chapter Nineteen

Suellyn pushed back the glass sliding doors to the wardrobe. With Tommy in the garden she decided to make herself useful by going through his clothes looking for anything to give away to the local charity store. As she bent over to pick up a pair of trousers which had fallen from a hanger, she noticed a cardboard storage box at the back of the wardrobe, hidden behind a pile of old blankets and a set of rusty golf clubs. Her curiosity was aroused. She wanted to know more about Tommy Dwyer - she wanted to know who he really was. She calculated that she wouldn't be disturbed for a while. Tommy enjoyed working in the garden and if he was left alone, he wouldn't reappear for hours.

Suellyn sat cross legged on the carpeted floor and began rummaging through the contents of the cardboard box. She found old school books belonging to Tommy, his parent's personal letters to each other, a few family snaps with people who looked like his extended family and bank books dating back to the late sixties and seventies. She casually opened them and noticed they were in Tommy's mother's name. At the bottom of the box, amongst a collection of bank statements, insurance bonds and other mundanities, she found a baby photo. The baby in the photo looked to be about seven months old, with chubby cheeks and a wide toothless grin. The child was sitting upright, straight-backed - William Phillips stared back at her.

'How did a baby photo of William end up amongst all this stuff?'

William at eight months was written on the back of the photo, scribbled in faded ink in her mother-in-law's scratchy hand writing. She recognised the photo from the one in the photo frame that Rose kept on her bedside table. Amongst Isabelle's papers, were letters from Rose thanking her for the money. What money? Suellyn noticed a bundle of letters held together by a rubber band at the bottom of the box. Written in Tommy's hand was an envelope addressed to Isabelle Dwyer. She removed the letter from the envelope, held it up to the light which was streaming through the bedroom window and began reading.

Dear Mother

I'm strapped for cash and I was hoping that you could help me out. I have plans to travel overseas and I need $50,000 immediately. I know you won't deprive me of the experience that international travel has to offer, so please transfer funds immediately to my bank account or I will be forced to act on our conversation yesterday, something I'm sure you wouldn't want me to do.

Your loving son as always,

Tommy

The menacing tone of the letter surprised even Suellyn. She wondered what he meant by 'acting on their conversation.' Was Tommy blackmailing his mother? Tommy's family was wealthy, but fifty-thousand dollars was still a lot of money in anyone's books. However, there was something else that bothered Suellyn. Tommy had told her that he had never travelled outside of Australia and that was why he was so keen to travel overseas now, before he got too much older. She wondered if Isabelle had given him the money and if she had, what he had done with it.

Suellyn reached deeper into the box and found another envelope – this one was addressed to Rose. She carefully broke the envelope's seal and unfolded the letter. She was surprised to find that it was a carbon copy. Carbon paper went out with the ark and Suellyn wondered if you could still buy it.

She assumed the original of the letter had been sent to Rose and wondered why Tommy's mother had gone to the trouble of keeping a copy. Was this her way of protecting herself from him? The contents of the neatly written letter startled her. Surely the Tommy she knew wasn't capable of what he was being accused of by his mother. Suellyn stood up from the floor. Pins and needles shot down her left leg and she massaged her calf with her hands until the blood began to flow. She quickly walked out of the bedroom down the hall towards the study and placed one of the letters on the glass plate of the fax machine and pressed the copy button. As she waited for the machine to warm up she watched Tommy through the window. He was down on his knees, his back was to her and a hessian bag of weeds was by his side.

After the fax machine spewed out a copy of the letters, she returned them to the envelopes and shoved the warm sheets of A4 paper into the pocket of her silk robe. She returned the letters to the box and began to flip through the yellowed pages of bank books. The books were filled with transfers written in smudged black ink, monthly withdrawals for several hundred dollars over a period of years, withdrawals recorded by bank tellers, probably long dead, the same amount, the same date, every month. She didn't find a withdrawal for fifty-thousand dollars recorded; perhaps Isabelle had money invested elsewhere…

Suellyn concentrated hard and gathered her thoughts. None of what she had just read made any sense. Tommy knew she was married to William. They had talked openly about William and Rose. Tommy had asked her questions about her husband and her mother-in-law when they first met and she remembered at the time she had been flattered by the fact that he wanted to know everything about her. She had been surprised by his interest in Rose. He had even asked her where she lived, her habits and about the state of her health. She'd not given it much thought at the time and assumed that he was just curious about her family but now it all made sense.

Both letters had a terrible tone to them and Suellyn's mind raced as she tried to think what she would or should do about the information that she had just discovered.

Chapter Twenty

Tommy removed his reading glasses, looked over the top of the newspaper he had been reading for the last ten minutes and gazed out across the ocean at a flock of seagulls, watching them as they swerved sharply and slipped between the waves. The surf was flat this morning and the sky was clear.

He wondered why he'd not heard from Suellyn. The last time he had spoken to her was when she phoned him last Wednesday and even then she sounded distant and preoccupied, as if she had something on her mind. There was a hint of anxiety in her voice, but that wasn't unusual for Suellyn, she was always anxious about something. Even so, he hoped she wasn't getting cold feet or feeling guilty about Rose. Disconnecting the power was a bit drastic he thought, but in the end, a result was what they were both after and who was he to judge her, he probably would have done the same thing given the circumstances. Suellyn was tough underneath all those hysterics. He liked that about her.

It was eleven-fifteen. The real estate agent said

he would drop by around eleven-thirty. The marketing campaign was on track and after a couple of open houses a young couple was interested in buying the beach house. Tommy had made up his mind a few weeks ago that it was time to move on after he discovered he was a beneficiary to Rose's estate. What a surprise that had been. The old girl must have felt guilty about inheriting what she knew was rightly his. With the sale of his house, the windfall from Rose's estate and the money Suellyn would eventually get from the sale of the house in Eden Street, they would be able to afford to live anywhere in the world. Tommy had suggested Spain but Suellyn wasn't keen on the idea, but perhaps now after everything that had happened, she would reconsider.

The couple was impressed with the house and the agent was confident that they would exchange contracts by the end of the following week. Tommy looked around him at the job he had ahead of him. He wasn't looking forward to packing up all his belongings but fortunately he was used to moving and most of the furniture in the house was rented anyway. Suellyn had already sorted through his clothes, but there were things he had to get rid of; starting with the contents of his bookcase and the two storage boxes in his wardrobe. The boxes were filled with childhood photos, letters and a collection of memorabilia his mother had sentimentally stashed away in her garage. The telephone rang. It was Suellyn.

'Hi Sues, how are things?'

'Things are fine Tommy, I just thought I'd let you know that it looks like we've got an interested buyer for the house in Eden Street. The real estate agent said that it didn't worry the buyers that Rose died in the kitchen, they're going to knock the house down anyway.'

'That's good news, so when am I going to see you? I've missed you.' Tommy smiled into the phone. His cheek dimpled.

'Things are a bit hectic here at the moment. Let's wait for things to quieten down, okay?' Suellyn breathed heavily into the mouth piece.

'Whatever you want, but listen, I've got some good news as well. A young couple inspected the house this morning. They're keen to buy it. Looks like all our plans are starting to take shape.'

'I knew it wouldn't take long for someone to snap it up. Having the beach at your back door really helps. All the same, I'm going to miss the place,' Suellyn said.

'So come up. What's stopping you? One last look for old times' sake.'

'I promise I'll come when I can get away. She hesitated, 'Look Tommy, I have to go, I think I heard William at the front door,' Suellyn lied. 'Speak to you soon.' Suellyn hung up and wondered what she was going to do about those letters. She was nervous and was having doubts. She was beginning to wonder who Tommy Dwyer really was and what he was capable of.

Suellyn was lying down on the lounge propped up against a couple of cushions, waiting for William to come home. She knew she had to tell him about the letters she found at the beach house. She stood up from the lounge and closed the sliding door. There was a market on today. Every weekend saw the influx of stall-holders peddling their wares, everything from organic goats' cheese to hand painted glass plates. Children were squealing; the sound of carnival rides and tuneless music slowly drifted up to the eighth floor of their apartment block. It was the only downside of living across from the beach, that, and the salt spray that drifted in from the ocean devouring everything in its path.

Tommy slid open the mirror robe. He leant in and dragged out the cardboard storage boxes from the back of the wardrobe. They were covered in a fine layer of dust. As he dragged the boxes out one by one across the tracks of the wardrobe, he knocked over his golf clubs. 'Bloody golf clubs.' Tommy couldn't remember the last time he played golf. His handicap never got below thirty in all the years that he'd played. He decided he would have a garage sale to get rid of the junk he had accumulated over the years.

He stacked the two storage boxes on top of each other and carried them out to the backyard where he had already set a small fire in the brick barbecue. The contents of the emptied box landed in a pile in front of him. Golden flames jumped and sparked into life as he added a small branch to the smoldering fire. The smell of eucalyptus filled the air as bank books and statements, black and white photos of his mother and father in happier times were engulfed by the flames. A life which was so distant now, he could hardly remember it. So much had happened since the day he found out about Rose and William Phillips. His face hardened. He remembered his father's dying wish for him to take care of his mother.

'No time for sentimentality now, Tommy old son,' he said quietly to himself. He sorted through letters and postcards and one by one he placed them on the fire. A whisper of wind sprung up and carried the ashes into the air. A burnt photo offering landed on his jumper. It was the face of his mother. It was just as well he wasn't superstitious he thought as he flicked the ash from his jumper. He scooped up the remainder of his mother's correspondence and added them to the fire. He wondered what had compelled him to keep the boxes, they held far too many memories. He picked up the second of the empty cardboard storage boxes and was about to throw it onto the fire when he noticed an envelope wedged into one of the corners of the box. He pulled at it and it came away. It was addressed to Rose Phillips in his mother's neat handwriting. Tommy turned the envelope over in his hands. It obviously had not been posted but the envelope had been opened and resealed. He tore at it and read the indigo blue words written on the unlined paper. His hands shook as he held the letter in both hands; deep frown lines formed on his forehead and his lips tightened. This was a carbon copy, so who had the original? Rose? And why had his mother decided to keep a copy of the letter? Who had she expected to read it? He threw the letter to the ground, trod on it and kicked it into roaring flames.

Chapter Twenty-One

William, we need to talk.'

'What is it now Suellyn?' William snapped. He was on his way to the beach. His full length wet suit fitted his body like a glove and a beach towel hung around his neck and over his broad shoulders. The wet suit outlined his taut muscled body and Suellyn followed the bumps and curves of his form right down to his tanned, naked feet.

'I've got something I want to show you before you go. It's to do with your mother.'

William placed his keys on the dining table and saw the anxious look on his wife's face. Suellyn was obviously frightened by something or someone. She was clutching sheets of crumpled paper in her hands. William took the letters from her and threw the towel over the back of the lounge and sat down to read them. Suellyn sat on the ottoman watching her husband closely for his reaction. Why didn't he say something, anything? The silence was physically painful.

'I'll have to hand these over to the police,' he said

eventually. 'These letters explain a lot. Where did you get them?'

'I found the original letter from Isabelle in your mother's bedroom after she died, the day you followed me, after we'd been to see the solicitor.' Suellyn still remembered the way William had slapped her face and the way he had sobbed afterwards. 'And I found a copy of the same letter at Tommy's house along with the letter Tommy wrote to his mother asking her for money.'

'So, this is what you were searching for? It's all starting to make sense to me know. You were trying to protect him weren't you? Is this why you wanted my mother out of the house, so you could find this letter and destroy it? Why show it to me now? What's changed?'

'No, you're wrong. I was trying to protect you. I admit I wanted to know what Tommy's involvement was in all of this. I was curious. Tommy told me that before his father died he had told him about the baby his mother had given away to Rose. But what Tommy didn't know was that Isabelle changed her will and left her entire estate to Rose. We both wanted to find out the full details of the inheritance and what Rose was planning to do with all the money. I just wanted to help Tommy get what was rightfully his. His mother should never have left her money to Rose. It wasn't right. Tommy tracked down her solicitor, that awful Bartholomew man, but he wasn't going to tell him anything apart from that he had acted for Rose regarding Isabelle's estate and that she had kept most of the paperwork at home. He knew a letter existed somewhere, outlining the reasons why Isabelle was leaving all of her estate to Rose. Knowing Rose, I knew the letter must have been somewhere in the house. You know what she was like William, she kept everything, she even had the first pay slip from when she worked at the dressmakers in the city before you were born.

I wanted to destroy any evidence that linked you and Tommy. I thought if I got her to move away I could search the house, find the letter and destroy it. I just wanted to protect you, I didn't want you to get hurt. I know what finding out about your father did to you. You have to believe me.'

'What was Tommy's involvement in all of this? Did he ever visit my mother, I mean Rose?'

'Tommy and I went to see Rose the day she died. I waited in the car outside while he went in to speak to her. He said he wanted to talk to her about his mother, to tie up a few loose ends.'

William's head was spinning. He looked at Suellyn and rubbed the back of his neck. 'And where did this letter from Tommy to his mother come from?'

'I found it at Tommy's place.' Suellyn was rubbing her arms nervously, she stood and walked towards William but he turned his back on her. 'William, I had no idea that Rose had written Tommy into her will.'

William spun around and raised his eyebrows.

'I didn't, really, you have to believe me. She probably did it to bring everything out into the open. It was like a clue, like the way you and Tommy both share the same middle name. She was probably too afraid to tell you the truth about Isabelle and that you had a brother. She knew how badly you took it when she tried to explain to you about the father she'd invented. I'm sure she was sick of all the lies but wanted to wait until after she was dead before you found out the truth. She was either too ashamed or too scared to tell you, especially after she had already tried to tell you the truth once before.'

William grabbed his keys and towel and slammed the apartment door behind him. He took the lift to the basement, grabbed his surfboard from the caged storage area and left the building by the fire exit which led out to the street in front of the building. The beach wasn't crowded today. With the first hint of cool weather it was only the most dedicated of surfers who took to the waves. William ran headlong into the surf and paddled out to the first break. He surfed at Manly Beach often enough that he recognised a few of the other surfers and acknowledged the ones he knew.

The water was a chilly eighteen degrees. The waves washed over him and cleared his mind. He sat upright on his board with his legs dangling beneath him and drifted for a while before he looked back over his shoulder towards the shore and watched as the waves cracked and thundered onto the beach. He watched a young girl who he didn't recognise, stretch up on her board like a cobra only to twist and flip over under the power of a freak wave.

William didn't stay long at the beach, he knew he had to call Jill Brennan and speak to her about the letters. Suellyn wasn't in the apartment when he returned an hour later and he was relieved that she had the sense to make herself scarce. He showered and walked out of the bathroom with a towel wrapped around his narrow waist. Water dripped from his hair. He picked up the cordless phone from the glass coffee table and selected Jill Brennan's phone number from the phone's directory and dialed.

It was Saturday. Jill Brennan's first weekend off in a month. The afternoon sea breeze blew her hair into her face and a few loose strands stuck to her lip gloss. The sun still had some warmth in it and the wind burnt her cheeks. The gravel track was crowded with people heading towards Bronte. She was standing behind the barrier at the edge of the cliff face, deep in thought, gazing out at the postcard views of the Pacific Ocean. Behind her at Bondi Beach, a mob of surfers sitting on their boards were waiting for a decent wave to carry them back to shore. A Westpac surf rescue helicopter flew overhead just as her phone rang. William wondered if she worked on Saturdays or if she had the weekends off.

She dug her phone out of the side pocket of her jeans and answered the call.

'Brennan speaking.' She raised her voice over the noise of the chopper and pressed her left hand over her ear to blot out the noise.

'Hello Jill, it's William Phillips. Sorry to disturb your weekend. What's that noise? Where are you?'

'A chopper's flying overhead. It'll be gone in a minute.' Jill waited for the sound of the rotors to fade. She screwed up her eyes and watched the helicopter bank to the right and head off down the coast. 'That's better,' she continued. 'Sorry about that, what were you saying?'

'I said I'm sorry for disturbing your weekend.'

'Oh, that's okay, I'm not doing anything special.'

'Look Jill, the reason for my call is because I've got some information that proves what I've thought all along, that Rose didn't commit suicide.'

Jill was surprised. There wasn't the slightest doubt in her mind that Rose Phillips's death had been anything but suicide. She thought William was just clutching at straws.

'Can I meet you somewhere?' William asked.

'Well, I'm at Bondi at the moment, standing on the edge of a cliff. Do you want to meet for a coffee?' she smiled into the phone.

'I'll be there in about forty minutes. I'll meet you at Café Utopia on Campbell Parade. Do you know it?'

'Yeah I know it. I'll see you soon then.'

Jill was puzzled. What information could William possibly have that was so urgent that he had to see her on her day off. She looked at her watch and made her way back down to the beach. She walked passed her car on the way to the café and fed the parking meter; enough to satisfy it's appetite for another two hours.

When she arrived at the café, Jill went straight to the bathroom and applied some makeup and brushed her hair. She wished now that she had worn her snug fitting jeans instead of the faded, baggy ones she was now wearing. Using some liquid soap from the soap dispenser, she dabbed at the grease stain from the bacon and eggs she'd had for breakfast that morning and looked at her reflection in the mirror.

'Well, that's the best I can do,' she said back at

herself. A toilet flushed and an overweight teenager with dyed jet black hair and spiky orange tips opened a cubicle door and joined her at the wash basin. She looked at Jill and smirked. Jill ignored her, embarrassed that she had been caught talking to herself.

She chose a table for two outside the café on the footpath so she wouldn't miss William when he arrived and picked up the menu tucked between the salt and pepper shakers and realised that she'd not eaten since breakfast. A shadow fell across the table as she tried to decide between the Caesar chicken salad or the pancakes with maple syrup. The aluminum chair next to her scraped against the concrete and she shielded her eyes against the sun as she looked up to see William Phillips towering over her. He pulled the chair away from the table and sat down.

'Waiting long?' he asked.

'No, just got here.'

William caught the attention of the waitress and ordered. 'Just coffee for me, short black,' he said.

'Same.' Jill decided she could do without the pancakes and the maple syrup. 'Well, William what's all this about. What's this information you've got to show me?'

William leant forward in his chair and pulled out the crumpled letters from the inside pocket of his jacket and pushed them across the table towards her. Jill laid the letters out flat and used the palm of her hand to smooth out the creases. He looked at her hands; they were small but strong, freckled and he noticed that her fingers were bare. William studied her carefully noticing the golden highlights in her hair as she read Isabelle's letter addressed to Rose. When she finished reading it, she transferred it to her left hand and began to read the second letter, the letter from Tommy to his mother, Isabelle Dwyer.

Jill frowned as she put the letters down on the table. 'Interesting. I'll show them to my boss and get his take on them.' She folded the letters and tucked them into an inside pocket of her backpack which was sitting between her feet beneath the table. 'Tell me William, what do you know about this Tommy Dwyer anyway? He's one of the beneficiaries to your mother's estate, right?'

'Yeah, but it's a long story. You got time to hear it?'

Jill sat back in the chair and smiled at William, 'All the time in the world.'

William ordered another coffee for both of them and began at the only place he knew where to begin - at the beginning. He described how his mother had raised him in a boarding house in an inner-city sub-urb; of the close relationship they had shared when he was young and how that changed once he crossed the divide and moved into the world of big business, big money and big demands. He told Jill of the regret he felt that he had abandoned his mother at a time when she had needed him most. He then went on to justify his actions, of how he felt that she was equally to blame because of her lack of honesty and how she wasn't prepared to meet him halfway. How she turned her back on him by not wanting to or not being capa-ble of understanding that he had moved on with his life, and that his life had evolved into something more complex and sophisticated than hers. He told her about the secrets and lies his mother had been guilty of, how she had picked up a photo of a soldier in a secondhand book store and cast him into the role of husband and father to cover up her moral indecency.

'So where does Tommy and Isabelle Dwyer come into all this?' Jill Brennan asked.

'Tommy Dwyer is my half-brother, he squirmed out of the woodwork after my mother died - just showed up out of nowhere.'

Jill shifted in her seat.

'Rose wasn't my biological mother - Tommy's mother, Isabelle was. Isabelle gave birth to me in London and took Rose along for the ride. Rose's name was recorded on my birth certificate. Rose was thirty and desperate to have a child of her own. She knew she would probably never have the opportunity again, time was running out for her. After looking after her elderly parents, the prospect of marriage and family seemed so out of reach.

The secrets and lies started with Isabelle. It was 1955, a different era, and she had her reputation to consider. She'd married a very wealthy man, with a large family fortune and she didn't want to have to explain to her husband how she managed to become pregnant when he wasn't capable of producing another heir. Two years after Tommy's birth, when they were trying to have another child, he came down with a severe case of mumps which made him sterile. But there's more to this sordid story. It also seems that my wife, Suellyn was having an affair with Tommy and they were planning to run away together. They were in this together. Tommy was trying to get Suellyn to find out what Rose was doing with the money she inherited from Isabelle. That's why Suellyn was so desperate to get Rose to move out of the house in Eden Street. She wanted Rose out of the way so she could have a thorough look through the house. When they found out that Rose made Tommy a beneficiary to the estate, well, that upset everything. Tommy realised that he was going to get his share after all. But that still wasn't enough he wanted the Eden Street house as well.

'But the house wouldn't be worth much though, would it?'

'Don't be put off with the way it looks. I know it's rundown but the land is worth at least twenty times the value of the house. The suburb's becoming popular with young families and they either want to knock the houses down and build two storey mansions or else renovate them, bring them back to their former glory.' William fiddled with the salt and pepper shakers on the table and looked across at Jill. 'But it's now got a whole lot more complicated with these letters turning up. Suellyn found them when she was rummaging through Tommy's things. He's got a beach house up the coast and he's just sold it. I think the two of them were about to do a runner, at least Suellyn was until these letters turned up. Seems like my wife has a conscience after all.'

'So what part do you think Suellyn played in all of this? Do you think she was capable of harming Rose?' Jill asked

'I really don't know. Suellyn can be impulsive and quick-tempered at times and she doesn't always consider the consequences of her actions. The fact that

Rose left a large part of her estate to Tommy might have swayed her to leave me and run off with Tommy. She tells me she's been unhappy in our marriage.' William rubbed the back of his neck and felt a huge knot. 'As far as Tommy goes though, he's a real concern. In my view, if you're looking for a motive as to why he would murder my mother, I mean Rose, you only have to remember that Isabelle cheated him out of his inheritance by leaving everything to her and he probably didn't have the faintest idea that Rose intended to leave almost half to him.'

The autumn sun had all but disappeared and shadows from the neighbouring buildings crept along the footpath to where William and Jill were sitting drinking their second cup of coffee. Jill began to shiver through her thin cotton shirt. The beach was almost deserted and the café was getting ready for the dinner crowd.

'I guess we should be making a move. I think we've outstayed our welcome,' Jill said as she looked over at the owner standing by the cash register.

After William paid for their coffees they left the café together and walked at a leisurely pace along Campbell Parade to where Jill had parked her car. Jill was cold and she crossed her arms across her body to try to warm herself. She didn't think to bring a coat when she left home earlier in the day.

'This is my car here.' Jill was relieved to see that she still had ten minutes on the meter. The parking rangers were notorious on this part of the strip. 'I'll be in touch William. We'll have to discuss these letters with your wife and do some digging around to find out the circumstances surrounding Isabelle's death.'

Jill unlocked the car and William held the door opened for her as she slipped in behind the wheel and threw her backpack onto the passenger seat. As she drove off she looked at William in the rear view mirror. He was standing on the footpath with his hands in his pockets staring out at the ocean.

Chapter Twenty-Two

'What's the low down on these two, Brennan?' Rimis asked.

Jill referred to her notebook. 'Okay, I'll start with William Phillips. He's a corporate counsel and works for a merchant bank in the high end of town. Ruthless in business, a workaholic by all accounts, but generally well respected and liked by his clients and work colleagues. Only son of Rose Phillips who is not his birth mother, father unknown. Lives with his wife Suellyn, married for about thirteen years, not so happily recently, I gather, no children. Apparently there was a fallout between William and Rose over a paternity matter. They weren't on speaking terms. The wife has had brief contact over the years with the deceased but apparently wanted her out of her Eden Street house. It is understood that she was the one responsible for disconnecting the electricity to the house and gave instructions to a local real estate agent, Ambah St John to sell it.' She paused and looked over at Rimis. 'She was the woman who found Rose's body.' He nodded. He remembered the young woman with the legs up to her neck and the blonde hair.

Jill continued. 'Not much is known about Suellyn Phillips, attractive, a social butterfly I suppose is a good description, flits around the place, likes the long, boozy lunches with the girls. If you don't mind me saying so Sarge, a bit of a selfish bitch is probably a good description. Known to hit the booze regularly and hard. Two counts of DUI over the past three years. Tommy Dwyer is on the scene and could be a person of interest. Dwyer's mother committed suicide about six months ago, interesting, same MO as the deceased.

'Okay, I've got the gist of it. The beneficiaries of Rose's estate are William Phillips, Thomas Dwyer Kevin Taggart, the next-door neighbour and Max Grey, an elderly neighbourhood gardener, correct?

'Yep.'

'I've met Mr Taggart. Strange fella that one. I've got my eye on him. Seems to have some sort of fascination for little old ladies.' He cocked his eyebrows. 'Most murder victims, if we are talking about murder here Brennan, are killed by people they know. Nine times out of ten, the murderer is someone who the victim knows, not a stranger. Murder is not usually a random act, the victim is someone who knows something, who has something, who's got money, get the picture? Always look at the family first though, that's usually where you'll find the perp, Brennan.'

'Here we are now, Sarge. Visitor parking is next to the entrance.'

Rimis parked in one of the visitor spaces and they walked to the front of the building. Brennan pressed the intercom. She introduced herself and the lock was released. Brennan and Rimis travelled in the lift to the eighth floor in silence. They flashed their IDs at Suellyn when she opened the front door and followed her as she led them into the lounge room where she invited them to take a seat.

'Can I get you something to drink? A coke, mineral water or something a little stronger?' Suellyn asked.

'No thanks, Mrs Phillips.' Rimis took a seat on a lounge and made himself comfortable. William walked into the room and looked straight at Jill, ignoring the hard-faced detective with her. Brennan introduced William to Nick Rimis.

'Nice place you've got here Mr and Mrs Phillips. Always fancied myself living by the beach - plan to take up surfing one of these days.' Rimis stood and flashed his ID card in William's face.

'With respect, let's get on with it Detective Sergeant, as you know this isn't a social call.' William looked at Jill and then back at Rimis.

'That's Detective Senior Sergeant,' Rimis scowled at William as he returned his ID to the inside pocket of his suit jacket. He didn't like the tone in William's voice and he wasn't accustomed to being told how to conduct an interview, especially by some smart-arsed barrister.

Jill led Suellyn away to the kitchen to make coffee.

'Let's make a start then Mr Phillips. For the record, please state your full name and address.' Rimis noticed the drinks cabinet and drifted towards it. He picked up the bottle of *Highland Park*. 'Nice drop William, expensive too.'

'Can we just get on with it?' Rimis turned around and faced William.

'By all means,' he replied.

William approached the sideboard where Rimis had been standing only a few moments earlier. 'My name is William Seymour Phillips; address Panorama Apartments, Marine Parade, Manly.' William poured himself a Scotch from the bottle and picked up his glass. He raised his eyebrows pointing the glass towards Rimis. The Detective Senior Sergeant shook his head.

'Mr Phillips, Detective Senior Constable Brennan has shown me, as you know, the letters written by Isabelle and Tommy Dwyer. That's why we're here of course. But before we get onto the letters, there are some questions I need to ask you. First, can you tell me a bit about the relationship between your late mother and your wife. From information gathered already, there seems to have been some sort of animosity between the two of them. Can you tell me about that Mr Phillips?'

'Well, I don't think there was any real animosity. At least no more than what you would expect between two strong-willed and headstrong women. Suellyn looked in on her occasionally to check to see if she was all right and coping on her own.'

'And how did your mother cope living on her own, Mr Phillips?'

'Well, it appears not very well, doesn't it? The house is in bad shape. It's pretty run-down and she was living there without electricity. But of course, you would already know that.'

'Can you tell me about your relationship with your mother and when you saw her last?'

'I didn't have a relationship with my mother I'm ashamed to say. I haven't seen her for years. We had a falling out over a family misunderstanding.'

Rimis scribbled down a few notes in his notebook and left William sitting on the lounge. He walked into the kitchen to where Jill and Suellyn were drinking coffee. Brennan was leaning against the kitchen bench, talking to Suellyn, playing the role of 'soft cop.' Brennan left Rimis to do his job and went to join William in the lounge-room.

'I'm not asleep. If that's what you were wondering.' William opened his eyes and unfolded his arms from across his chest. His feet were resting on the coffee table and his legs were stretched out in front of him. Jill smiled and sat down in the lounge chair opposite him. The apartment was tastefully decorated. The walls were covered in original artwork, rich red and royal blue Persian rugs were thrown across the glossy white tiled floors. The painting above the dining table was an Arthur Boyd. The pair sat in silence, neither of them knowing what to say to each other.

Rimis began his questioning. 'Mrs Phillips, I'm going to have to ask you some questions about the death of Rose Phillips. Anything you say or do will be recorded. Do you understand that?'

Suellyn replied that she did, surprised that she was being given a formal caution.

'Can you tell me your full name and address for

the record, and your movements between the hours of one pm and seven pm on the 20th May this year?'

'Is this really necessary?' she asked as she picked over a bowl of pistachios on the bench.

'Yes, Mrs Phillips, this is necessary. This is a police investigation and we are trying to establish the facts.'

'We're supposed to be discussing these letters I found, aren't we? Isn't that why you're here?'

'Please just answer my question Mrs Phillips.'

'I don't have to answer him do I, William?' Suellyn called out to William at the top of her voice. 'Look, it's up to you Mrs Phillips, if you don't want to talk to me here, we can take you down to the station and ask the same questions there.'

Before Rimis and Brennan arrived, William had warned her that she should just state the facts and tell the police everything she knew. He warned her not to get emotional.

'Okay, okay, if you really must know, I was out with a friend. We went shopping all afternoon and then went on to have dinner at Eccos in the city. I remember the date because it was Rosalind's birthday.'

Suellyn picked up her coffee mug and realising it was almost empty, swirled the burnt coffee grinds around in the cup before putting it back down on the bench. She glared at Rimis. 'Are you accusing me of something Detective? I think it's Tommy Dwyer you should be speaking to, not me.'

'Mrs Phillips, the questions I'm asking are all relevant to our investigations. We have to carry out the enquiry into your mother-in-law's death and we have to do it as we see fit, we have to explore all the possibilities. Now, can you tell me about Tommy Dwyer and what your relationship with him was at the time of your mother-in-law's death?'

'That's a personal question. For Christ's sake, who doesn't know about me and Tommy Dwyer?' Suellyn corrected her posture and slapped her thighs hard with the palms of her hands. She stormed across to where Nick Rimis was standing on the other side of the kitchen and looked him square in the eye. 'Can I ask you something now Detective Senior Sergeant?' Suellyn emphasized the *Senior Sergeant*.

'Certainly Mrs Phillips, please, go right ahead,' he replied in a frosty voice.

'Is this how you go about investigating a death? Asking uninvolved people unnecessary questions?'

'Mrs Phillips, I don't have to justify our investigation to you. We'll be conducting interviews with numerous people who were associated with Rose Phillips.'

'Well, I'm not going to help you do your job. You go figure out who killed her if you think she was murdered. And I want those letters back,' she screeched. 'Tommy didn't kill her, he wouldn't do something like that. I know him too well. I made a mistake of accusing him of... well, I don't really know what I was accusing him of. I probably shouldn't have involved William in all of this. I'm so mixed up, I wish I...'

'Suellyn! That's quite enough. Stop raising your voice, it won't get you anywhere.' William was standing in the kitchen doorway. He reached out and grabbed his wife by the shoulders and shook her.

'All right, Mr Phillips.' Rimis thought it was time to diffuse the situation. He lowered his voice and put on his 'good cop' voice. 'Mrs Phillips this probably isn't a good time for you. You are obviously upset by your mother-in-law's death but this is an ongoing investigation and we may need to talk with you at some later time.'

'You should be investigating real suspects instead of wasting your time on us detective. We were Rose's only family you know. Now, is that all?' Suellyn demanded. 'My husband will show you and your colleague to the door.'

Nick Rimis realised he was wasting his time trying to get any sense from this strung out woman. He felt sorry for her husband and wondered how he put up with her. Rimis looked at William almost sympathetically when he saw the look on his face. 'Thanks for your time Mr Phillips. We'll be in touch soon.'

William showed the two detectives to the door and closed it firmly behind them.

'Well, that went well didn't it, Sarge?' Jill said sarcastically as she pressed the call button for the lift.

'My gut feeling is that there is a lot more to Suellyn Phillips than what she wants us to think. If you ask me, I'd say what we just witnessed was a clever piece of stage acting.'

'Do you really think she was acting, or is she just a neurotic bitch?'

'Now, now Brennan, language. And to answer your question whether I think she was acting, only time will tell. But one thing I do know, we need to pay Mr Dwyer a visit and it might be a good idea to get hold of the post mortem records for Mrs Dwyer.'

'I'm one step ahead of you, Sarge. I've already put

in a requisition for the PM records. We should have them by tomorrow.'

Chapter Twenty-Three

William Phillips was a creature of habit. On Sunday evenings, except when he was out of town on business, he took the lift down to the gym located on the first floor of the Panorama Apartment block and swam thirty laps of the twenty-five metre pool. The centre was equipped with a pool, spa and steam room. Down a corridor behind another set of doors was the gym, equipped with treadmills, rowing machines and exercise bikes.

Bryan and Julie Sykes were regular Sunday-nighters at the gym and ignored the Strata Body notice glued to the wall. The Strata Corporation by-laws placed a prohibition on alcohol, the use of glass containers within the pool area, unnecessary running, excessive splashing, nude bathing and the presence of children under the age of sixteen who were not under the direct supervision of an adult. There was only one by-law they didn't take exception to, and that was the restriction of unsupervised children. But as William knew, some rules were meant to be broken and he turned a blind eye to the couple's drinking, especially when they were considerate enough to bring along an extra champagne flute for him.

William inserted his pass key into the electronic reader and the glass door clicked open. The centre was deserted. He had the place to himself and he was relieved. He didn't feel like socialising with Bryan and Julie tonight. He stripped off his track suit top and pants and placed his towel and keys on the timber bench under the sign that said 'no diving'. His swimming goggles slipped easily over his head, fitting snug against his face. With his swimming costume adjusted and the white cord tucked neatly into them, he dived into the deep end of the pool. As his face broke the surface, his body slid effortlessly through the water and he relaxed as his powerful arms and legs settled into a swimmer's rhythm. Stroke after effortless stroke his breathing kept in time with his heartbeat. Up and down, lap after lap, he glided through the pool. When he rolled into his thirtieth lap, he caught sight of someone standing by the edge of the pool. When the tips of his fingers touched the northern end of the pool, he planted his feet on the bottom, turned and looked behind him. Whoever was watching him, wasn't there now.

He flicked his head to one side, a shower of water droplets sprayed into the air just like a wet dog shaking itself after a bath. His broad shoulders took his weight as he eased his body out of the water. He snatched up his towel from the bench, dried off and headed towards the steam room.

He punched the green start button next to the door with his fist and closed the heavy door behind him. Cedar timber slats poked into his spine as he flattened his body against the bench. With his knees bent, he rolled up his towel to form a pillow and tucked it under his head. The room was already warm and it wasn't long before the temperature gauge began to climb to sixty-five degrees Celsius. William felt the effects of the heat and knew it was doing his body good. Rivulets of condensation dribbled down the walls and across the small square boxed window on the steam room door. Beads of sweat trickled down his body as he set the alarm on his waterproof watch for ten minutes. William tilted his head back, closed his eyes and felt all the muscles in his body relax.

Ten minutes later his alarm beeped, slowly, quietly at first, then it escalated in pitch, singing off-key to William, urging him to take notice, to open his eyes, to wake up. He was slow to move, he opened his eyes, his breathing was laboured. As he sat upright, he was immediately overcome by nausea, his chest tightened but he managed to get to his feet and reach for the timber handle on the back of the door. He pushed at it, but it wouldn't budge. He pushed again.

The door remained firmly shut. He looked around for an emergency button. He'd never paid much attention to the workings of the steam room before, but now he wished he had. A timber bucket was tucked away in the corner of the room. He heaved. After he regurgitated the soupy contents of his stomach into the bucket, he wiped his mouth with his towel and wished he had some water to rinse away the foul taste of vomit and bile.

Wasn't there some safety mechanism that was

supposed to come into play here? William banged on the glass window with his fists. He was sure there was an automatic timer switch that was supposed to cut in after ten minutes. Surely it wasn't on the outside of the door. 'Fucking door!' he yelled, as he kicked it with the last of his remaining strength.

He yelled at the top of his voice. Where was his mobile phone? He realised he'd left it with his clothes by the pool. William pressed his face up hard against the window. But he knew no one would hear him, after all it was Sunday night, the pool complex was deserted. He wished now that Bryan and Julie had come to the pool. They were always here on Sunday nights. Where were they?

William sat down on the floor. His skin was on fire, his throat was dry. The humidity of the steam room was overwhelming and as he sat quietly with his towel wrapped around his head, he began to pray. Not that William Phillips was a religious man but he had run out of options. What else was there left to do? Praying for someone to enter the pool complex and rescue him was all that he could think of to get out of the mess he was now in. He didn't want to die, not like this, but William knew that was exactly what was about to happen if someone didn't rescue him soon. Suellyn had gone out for the evening and he didn't even know if she was planning to come home.

William's heart rate was rising, his core temperature was soaring. In desperation he searched under the bench looking for the pipe which injected steam into the room. He heard it hissing, spluttering. Would he reach it in time before he passed out? Sweat was dripping off him in bucket loads and was streaming down his chest. His body was cooking, he felt like a pig roasting on a spit. The pain was excruciating, his skin was turning lobster-red. He sensed that he was about to lose consciousness. His head fell forward, his body rolled into a tight ball. A large crack sounded as his head landed hard against the tiled floor.

William had no idea that his prayers had been answered as he lay unconscious on the floor. The shut off switch sprang back and the switch turned off. A limp strip of grey electrical duct tape dangled from the switch.

Jock Kelly came on duty five days a week, Monday to Friday, at six am sharp. It was now six-ten, Monday morning. It had taken him ten minutes to unlock his office in the basement, check his emails and take the flight of stairs to the first floor. As he walked briskly towards the Fitness Centre the first thing he noticed was the typed notice taped to the door - *Closed for Maintenance.* He grabbed the notice and screwed it up into a ball and wondered who the practical joker was.

The affable Scot had been the building superintendent at the Panorama Apartments for almost five years. He was meticulous in the way he carried out his duties and he shook his head when he saw the pile of clothing on the bench at the northern end of the pool and he wondered what had gone on the night before.

Jock picked up the set of keys and the mobile phone which was tucked under a pair of grey tracksuit pants and realised he would have to put the car park key through the DKS reader to see who the keys belonged to. The mobile phone was dead.

Jock cast his eye around for anything else that looked amiss as he made his way towards the edge of the pool. It was all clear. Checking the pool was one of the items on his mental checklist. Last summer an elderly resident suffered a heart attack while doing laps and Jock had discovered his body spread-eagled at the bottom of the pool.

But everything seemed in order today and for that, Jock Kelly was grateful. He turned to leave knowing he still had to inspect the rest of the building before returning to the basement to check the garage roller doors and put the key tag through the reader to find out who the clothes and mobile phone belonged to. The garage doors had been playing up recently and he was fed up with being called out late at night to let someone into or out of the building.

He checked his watch. If he hurried he'd make it across the Bridge before the traffic got too heavy. He stopped as he turned to leave. Something had caught his attention. He looked at the wall next to the steam room and tried to make sense of the strip of grey electrical tape dangling from the automatic shut off switch. When he reached the steam room he tugged at its heavy timber door and wondered why it wouldn't open. He looked down at his feet and saw the thin wedge of timber which had been placed under the door. He kicked it away with his foot and looked through the window.

'What tha fawk?'

William Phillips was lying on his side on the floor, unconscious or perhaps dead. The white floor tiles where he lay were smeared with a pool of sticky blood. He pushed against the door, it opened and he bent down and shook William violently. 'Wake up marn for Christ's sake!' he yelled.

William opened his eyes, groaned and looked up at Jock.

'You took your bloody time.'

Chapter Twenty-Four

Isabelle Dwyer was frightened. She and Tommy had never been close, but their relationship had deteriorated since Charles had died. Tommy had become morose, his mood had spiraled downwards sending him windmilling into a deep well of depression. He'd turned on Isabelle, blaming her for his father's death, lashing out at her with vicious threats. Isabelle didn't know how long it would be before he would lose control completely and strike out. At one point she had her suspicions that he may have discovered her dirty secret. But how could he have known? Charles didn't know about Rose and William. Or did he? Isabelle was now beginning to wonder.

Isabelle knew that Tommy was jealous of the love his father had for her and knew he couldn't see anything in her character worth loving. Tommy didn't particularly like women, especially older women, he thought they were vile and pathetic.

When Tommy learned from his father what his mother had done, he went into a rage. His father pleaded with him to forgive her and insisted that he take care of her after he was gone. Tommy promised his father that he would, and he did, but in his own way. Two hours after their conversation he sent her a letter and demanded fifty-thousand dollars from her.

Within a week of his father's death he travelled interstate for two weeks. When he returned to the family home he sat with Isabelle at the kitchen table and plied her with gin and antidepressants and didn't listen when she pleaded with him to call an ambulance.

He left her dying, satisfied that a part of the debt Isabelle owed him and his father had been settled, and walked away from the house. He waited for an hour before hailing a taxi. Obscured by the dark shadows, seated in the back seat of the taxi, he arrived at Kingsford Smith International Airport. He didn't say a word when he paid the taxi driver in cash.

The next day, on the other side of the world, he waited half an hour before his bag finally appeared on the luggage carousel at Charles de Gaulle airport. The woman behind the Europcar rental counter didn't pay much attention to the man with the strange accent. She accepted his euros in exchange for the keys to a black, two door Peugeot. He placed the keys in his pocket and caught a shuttle bus to the rental car pickup area and headed out onto the A1 towards Gonesse. He had a long, lazy trip ahead in which to plan and fine-tune the next stage of his revenge. He travelled from country to country, from small village to small village, never staying in one place long enough for the authorities to find him. Six months later he returned home to learn that his mother had committed suicide and her estate had been dealt with by the executor, a Mr Martin Bartholomew. He disguised his rage when he learned from Martin Bartholomew that his mother's entire estate had been left to a long time friend, a Mrs Rose Phillips and disguised his relief when he learnt that the Coroner's findings were that her death was a result of a combination of alcohol poisoning and an overdose of prescription medication; a case of suicide brought about by the loss of her beloved husband Charles and the sudden disappearance of her only son.

My Dear Rose

I hope this letter finds you well. I was so pleased to receive your letter. Thank you for your sympathetic and kind words but the doctors have told me that Charlie won't last the week. He is very frail but still manages to understand what is going on around him. I will miss him, he has been a good husband to me and a good provider. I know that Tommy will miss him too, of course, because they did everything together before he fell ill. They were more like brothers than father and son.

Rose dear, it is because of Tommy that I felt that I had to write to you. A week ago Tommy came to me and told me that he knew all about Father Patrick and our little arrangement regarding William. I don't know how he found out, but he did, and he has been blackmailing me ever since. He asked me to give him fifty-thousand dollars to stop him from going to Charlie and telling him everything.

I just couldn't have Charlie knowing about William and going to his grave with such a terrible opinion of me. I was also worried that at the last moment he might decide to change his will in favour of Tommy and leave me without a cent.

Speaking of wills, Tommy asked me to show him mine just the other day, which I thought very strange. He knows that Charlie has left everything to me of course and I am sure he is expecting to inherit everything once I die. Tommy promised that he wouldn't tell anyone about William if I gave him the fifty-thousand dollars and he also promised that he would never raise the subject again. I hate to say it Rose, but I don't trust my son.

I hope you have fared better with Billy. I have never been very close to Tommy as you know, so I have decided to change my will. What a surprise is in store for him when I die and he is left nothing. I have made an appointment with your lovely solicitor friend, Mr Bartholomew, because I have decided to make you the sole beneficiary to my estate. You may die before me of course and in that case my assets will go to my two favourite charities.

My private funds that I kept from Charlie all these years are almost depleted mainly because of the recent fifty-thousand dollar payment to Tommy and the years I supported Billy. But I'm not really worried about that; that was the arrangement we agreed to and I stuck to it, didn't I?

Rose, do with the money what you will, but I must warn you that Tommy will not be pleased when he finds out that you have inherited everything. Perhaps you can introduce him to his half-brother and with Billy being a barrister and everything, it might just be for the best that the truth finally comes out into the open after all these *years. Don't judge me too harshly, you know what I'm like, I always was one to stir the pot!*

I haven't been very well lately and I am tired, but don't worry, I don't intend to kick the bucket anytime soon. Tommy tells me he is going overseas with the money I gave him, good riddance to bad rubbish I say. I really don't know where I went wrong with him. I know I must sound unkind, but you don't know my Tommy.

Anyway take care and I will keep you informed about Charlie. I don't expect you to come to the funeral because that would be too complicated and I wouldn't want Tommy asking any more questions. I will miss my husband, he was always so understanding.

Keep well
Your friend, Isabelle

Rimis returned the letter to the file marked *PHILLIPS-Rose FILE NO 234/088B* and placed it on his desk. He leant back in his chair, stretched out his legs in front of him and rubbed his face with the palms of his hands. 'This case just gets more complicated, Brennan. I think after reading these letters again that you've probably come to the same conclusion as I have. The Phillips case has just turned into a homicide enquiry.'

Jill nodded. 'It gets worse Sarge. Suellyn Phillips's alibi doesn't stack up. Rosalind Duncan said she did go shopping with Suellyn but she rushed off around three-thirty after she received a phone call. They *had* planned to go to Eccos but they didn't end up going.

Suellyn told Rosalind that she had something important she had to do.'

'I think it's time for us to go and pay Tommy Dwyer a visit to see what he has to say about all of this. What's the name of the hotel he's staying at?'

'The Barclay, Sarge.'

Chapter Twenty-Five

Rose unlocked the front door, parked her canvas shopping trolley against the wall in the hallway and placed her beret on the hatstand as she always did when she returned home from her shopping trips. Her hair had not been washed for weeks and it sat flat like an oily rag against her skull. She walked into the bedroom and sat down on the edge of the bed to remove her lace up shoes from her swollen feet. Rose had two pairs of slippers, a pink pair and a blue pair. Because her feet were so swollen today, she slipped her feet into the pink pair which was one size larger. She peered over her glasses at her swollen ankles. The hot, angry skin looked as if it was about to split like the casing on pork sausages suddenly thrown into a frying pan full of fat.

Her calloused toes were cracked and split and there was a thin line of dirt wedged under the nails. She tried to get the blood pumping through her scarred veins but Rose knew it was like trying to start a fire by rubbing two sticks together - an almost impossible task. Her circulation was shot, like everything else in her life. Rose steadied herself by holding onto the edge of the bed and stood up slowly. She shuffled across the floorboards into the kitchen, dragged the teapot down from the shelf and threw in a fist full of tea leaves. The chair scraped against the floor as she pulled it slowly out from the kitchen table. She waited for the kettle to boil and thought about Suellyn. She knew she was responsible for disconnecting the power. Who else would have done such a thing? Fortunately, she hadn't thought to disconnect the gas. She could still make herself a cup of tea.

The kettle whistled and sang to her. The sound brought her back to the present and reminded her of what Suellyn had planned for her. Tears suddenly formed and dribbled down through the valleys and crevasses of her sagging jawline, stopping before cascading over the edge of her chin and onto the puckered skin of her neck.

Rose had always assumed that she would live out her remaining days quietly in the rundown house in Eden Street. She never imagined for a moment that Suellyn would sell the house while she was still well enough to live there. During the past few months her daughter-in-law had tried to cajole, convince and bully her into moving to a retirement village. Stubbornly, she had refused to budge, she wasn't going anywhere. Rose decided that she would stay right where she was and make Suellyn sorry, one way or another, make her pay for her ruthless treatment of her. She hoped William would discover at last the sort of woman Suellyn really was and hold her accountable for the suffering she had caused. Perhaps he would even blame himself for his neglect of her.

It was cold inside the house and Rose didn't bother to remove her coat. The days were becoming shorter, colder and soon it would be winter. She rubbed her hands together, poured herself another cup of tea and reached into the cupboard next to the sink. She pulled out a packet of iced biscuits and placed them on the table.

Since receiving Isabelle's letter and learning a short time afterwards from Martin Bartholomew of her friend's death, she knew it wouldn't be long before Tommy Dwyer came calling. She wasn't planning to be around when he knocked on her door. She didn't want to come face to face with Isabelle's elder son.

She sat down and tucked herself into the kitchen table and wondered what would happen after she died. Would William and Suellyn come to the house? Would they poke around in her cupboards? They wouldn't find anything of value of course, but Suellyn might begin to wonder if there was a family heirloom or some unknown bank account long forgotten, hidden or misplaced in the back of one of her cupboards. Rose knew that once your loved ones were dead and buried, those left behind were impatient to return things to the way they were, to restore the balance, to tie up any loose ends and pack off the deceased's best suit or their favourite pair of 'going out shoes' to the local charity store. She knew this because that was exactly what she had done when her mother and father had died.

Her parents died within a week of each other, which was convenient for them and convenient for her. Her mother had kept a neat, orderly house and not having many possessions, the task had not been difficult. Rose breezed in and walked straight out again of her parent's modest two bedroom rented house with what she thought she could use. A handful of books for William, an assortment of childhood photos and the big brown soup pot that she had always admired. It was still sitting in the same cupboard next to the stove where her mother had always kept it. The rest she sold to a second hand dealer and pocketed the money.

Mother and son had not spoken for years and now as Rose sat alone in her kitchen, she felt sorry for herself and sorry for her son. He wasn't a bad or even an evil man, but he was a person who wasn't able to forgive. Some people aren't capable of forgiveness, life had taught her that. They are hurt by a selfish act and carry that hurt with them for the rest of their lives, assuming the person who hurt them was not be trusted, was not worthy of their love. They weren't able to move on, to forget and put the past behind them. Rose had always thought this was a strange way of thinking and a cruel way to treat a fellow human being - a lapse in consideration or judgement by any person shouldn't taint their character for the rest of their lives. Rose knew William was ashamed of her working class background and her hermit like existence. She had been waiting patiently for years, hoping that he would contact her but was not surprised that he never did. William Phillips was a proud and arrogant man.

As Rose searched for a teaspoon in the cutlery drawer she found the business card that Suellyn had left on the kitchen table the day she had told her she was selling the house. She held it up to the light. Her fingers shook as she held the card and tried to read the name which was printed in embossed letters on the stark cardboard. Her eyes squinted. Ambah St John. Such a strange sounding name she thought as she laid it down on the table next to her medication.

A dark shroud suddenly enveloped her, like winter itself, it weighed heavily on her. Old age was drowning her in a river of forgetfulness, she was slowing down, years of regret and sorrow seeped into her veins and entered every cavern of her existence. Her eyesight was failing and the fact that she'd not paid the gas bill didn't bother her anymore; nothing mattered. She stroked Astrid and put her in the laundry with a bowl of cat food and hoped that whoever found her would take her home and look after her, but then again, she was old, who would want an old incontinent cat who vomited inside the house?

Rose placed the small, round pills, one by one into her mouth. Rather than swallowing a whole mouthful of them, she flushed each one down individually with a mouthful of Earl Grey tea. She thought by doing this, she could always change her mind, but with each pill, she became more resolute. She pulled her coat around her wasted body and picked up the business card with the strange sounding name on it and closed her eyes. The card fell from her hand and floated gently to the floor.

The house was silent apart from Astrid's occasional soft miaowing and the kitchen clock which ticked loudly as the sun slipped lower in the sky. It was five pm and it had only been a few minutes, not long enough for the pills to take effect, when Rose heard a loud knock at the front door. She didn't move. There it was again. Her legs twitched, slowly at first and then she moved her head. Her eyes opened and for a moment she wondered if she had imagined the knock. Had she been dreaming? Her first instinct was to ignore whoever it was. Then she changed her mind. She would deal with them and send them on their way so that she could get on with the business of dying.

The kitchen table creaked from her weight as she stood up and placed her hands on the side of the table to steady herself. She looked at the clock. It was only a few minutes past five. She shuffled down the hallway towards the front door, past her shopping trolley and the hatstand where her beret with the yellow pom-poms was hanging. 'Who is it?' she asked.

There was no answer. Rose wondered if her visitor had heard her. She called again and pulled out her spectacles from her coat pocket and with trembling hands placed them on her nose. 'Who's there?' Still, there was no answer. Rose opened the door. She looked up at the man standing in the doorway.

He was taller than she had expected, his eyes were dark, his lips thin and his grey, wavy hair was receding from his high forehead. He was unshaven and wore a heavy overcoat. A plastic shopping bag sat at his feet.

'Hello Mrs Phillips. We haven't met before, but you were very good friends with my mother. My name is Tommy, Tommy Dwyer, Isabelle's son.'

Rose took a step closer and looked at the man standing in front of her. She looked at his face and into his eyes and recognised the family resemblance.

She had been expecting him, but why had he decided to come now? Against her better judgement she invited him in and directed him towards the kitchen. 'The kitchen's through there,' she said, pointing with a bony finger.

There was a draught coming from somewhere and the house smelt of cat piss, dust and mildew. He was surprised, this was not what he had expected, not what he had expected at all.

'I'll put the kettle on and we can have a cup of tea.' Rose struck a match and held it against the gas. The match died before she had a chance to light the candle in the middle of the table. She struck another and held it to the wick and it took hold.

A broad grin appeared on Tommy's lips. Old people and their cups of tea he thought to himself.

'I brought a bottle of Scotch with me. I thought we could enjoy a glass while we talked over old times. I know you must have a lot to tell me about my mother, seeing you two were friends for such a long time.'

'I'm sorry, but I don't drink alcohol dear. I'm a TT, a teetotaller, always have been, always will be. I'm glad to say I never acquired the taste for wine or spirits. The devil's work my mother used to say.' Tommy's demeanour suddenly changed. He realised this was going to be a lot harder than he thought. He didn't know that Rose didn't drink and was annoyed with Suellyn for not having told him, annoyed with himself for not having asked. Rose busied herself with the tea making. He sat down at the kitchen table on a high backed chair and looked at the paper thin slivers of paint which hung from the ceiling and at the timber window frame which was missing a pane of glass. Two packets of prescription pills lay on the table and Tommy noticed that all the blisters had been popped. Just as well he brought his own supply of Sinequan and Noctamid he thought. While they waited for the kettle to boil, their polite small talk turned from the weather to Isabelle Dwyer.

'My mother never told me about you, Mrs Phillips. It wasn't until after she died that your name came up on the radar so to speak. I was surprised when I learnt that she left everything to you when she died. I didn't realise she held you in such high regard.'

'But she told me all about you, Tommy Dwyer.' Rose sat down at the table with the teapot, a cracked cup and a small milk jug. A sugar bowl sat on the table next to a jar filled with jelly beans. Ring mark stains from past teacups interrupted the intricate pattern of orange blossoms on the brown vinyl tablecloth.

Now that she was sitting across from him, Rose took her time to study his features. As he was Isabelle's elder son it was natural that he would have her unruly hair, as did William. She wondered as she looked at the streaks of grey through his once dark hair, if her Billy had also begun to go grey. His dark eyes looked cruel, unlike Billy's whose eyes were soft and kind. Tommy crossed his arms in front of his chest, leant forward and rested his elbows on the table. He was close enough to her that she could smell his aftershave. It was sickly sweet and his breath was stale and frosty.

'I won't have tea. Do you mind if I open this bottle of Scotch instead?' He pulled the bottle from the plastic shopping bag which was sitting on the floor next to him, placed it on the table and twisted the lid with his right hand and held the neck of the bottle with his left. Rose noticed his gloved hands holding the bottle and was reminded of her father who had been a heavy drinker and a bully. Reminded of the lingering smell and the violence that always followed when the bottle was empty. Of the muffled sobbing that drifted into her room in the middle of the night and of her mother's red swollen eyes the following morning.

Rose blinked. 'Sorry, what did you say dear?' Rose was having trouble focusing on what Tommy was saying.

'Do you mind if I have a drink?' he repeated.

Rose waved her hand at him dismissively. 'No, of course not. I'll get you a glass.' Rose walked over to the cupboard above the kitchen sink and reached inside. She pulled out one of the dozen empty jam jars which she used as water glasses and looked inside the glass to check if it was clean before offering it to him. Tommy poured the Scotch from the tall bottle and Rose sat silently watching as the straw coloured liquid streamed into the jam jar. The house was quiet apart from the ticking of the kitchen clock.

Rose looked at Tommy's hands again as he poured the pale yellow liquid. It was cold, but surely not cold enough to warrant gloves. It wouldn't be winter until next month and she wondered if he suffered from a skin condition. The jam jar sat in the middle of the table. Rose poured herself a cup of tea and took a small sip from her teacup before placing it back on the saucer, next to the opened bottle of Scotch.

'I wasn't expecting visitors, but I have some iced biscuits if you would like one.'

Tommy ignored her and stared past her. Rose noticed his icy cold stare. He lacked the soft features of his mother and Rose thought he may have resembled his father. She had never met Charlie Dwyer so she couldn't say, but there was something disquieting about this man who was sitting across from her.

'Mrs Phillips, I think you should have a drink.'

'I'm waiting for it to cool down dear, I don't like to drink tea when it's too hot. I always burn my tongue.'

Tommy placed his gloved hand gently on her wrist. 'Drink the Scotch Mrs Phillips, it's *Highland Park,* it's excellent quality.' He picked up the jam jar and placed it in front of her. 'I insist.'

'I told you, I don't drink...'

'You see Rose, I can call you Rose, can't I?'

Rose nodded.

Tommy stood and walked over to the kitchen bench. He turned, and said quietly, 'Rose, we can either do it the easy way or the hard way. You can drink my Scotch in a ladylike fashion, or else, I can pour it down your scrawny throat.'

As Rose looked at the glass of Scotch, Tommy reached into the cutlery drawer and selected a sharp knife. He returned to the table and waved the blade menacingly in her face, close enough to her that she smelt his breath. It was sour and she turned her head away from him.

'Come on Rose, have a drink.' The good humour Tommy had shown earlier had disappeared, his lips stretched back over his teeth to reveal his red, fleshy gums.

'No, I wont you awful man, I told you, I don't drink.' She pushed the jam jar back across the table. Tommy straddled the chair and pressed his face into hers.

Rose winced as she looked at the knotted vein throbbing in his temple. He picked up the jar, gently held her chin and held it to her lips. Flashing lights blinked behind her eyes as she emptied the glass. Tommy refilled it. She didn't like the taste, she didn't like Tommy Dwyer. Her hands trembled, her eyes began to water.

'Suellyn was right. You are a stubborn old biddy.'

The combination of the whisky and the pills was taking effect. What did he want from her anyway? Didn't he know that she was going to die?

'Drink up Rose, and I'll tell you why I'm here.'

She looked at Tommy through dazed eyes, her body was swaying even though she was seated. He held the jar to her lips again and pinched her nose gently. She drank, but didn't swallow. She coughed and the Scotch spurted from her mouth and trickled down her chin.

Tommy pulled out the packet of Sinequan from his pocket. He would start with these first. He opened the blisters and emptied the tablets onto the table. He used the flat blade of the knife to ground the tablets into a powder then added them to the glass. 'You see Rose, I'm mighty upset my mother saw fit to leave her entire estate to you, especially after all the trouble I went to in order to kill her.'

The alcohol was fermenting and bubbling in her brain, her vision blurred and she had a strong desire to vomit. She looked at Tommy or was it Billy? They were so alike. 'Dora, is that you? Look after Billy.' Beads of sweat erupted on her skin. 'Billy, Billy, I'm sorry.' She looked again, but it wasn't Billy, it was Isabelle's boy, Tommy, and what was that he just said? Did he say *kill her, he killed Isabelle?* 'Oh, God I'm going to die,' she said in a groggy voice which she didn't recognise as her own. She watched Tommy's lips move and tried to make sense of the words he was mouthing.

'I don't..., don't..., really want to die.'

'Come on Rose, drink up, one last drink,' Tommy said, as he lifted her chin with his thumb. He dribbled more of Suellyn's expensive Scotch between her thin, bloodless lips and down her throat. She swallowed and looked up at Tommy Dwyer realising he would be the last person she would see before she died. Her eyes rolled back into her head before falling forward onto the table with a loud thud. He pulled her head up by the oily roots of her hair and then let it fall back down again onto the table, and he was satisfied. She was out cold, he felt her pulse, it was weak, she would be dead soon. He wiped the table down with a dishcloth, rinsed it and emptied the remainder of the contents of the bottle down the sink. He rinsed the jam jar and the whisky bottle and left them to drain in the red plastic drainer next to the kitchen sink. He took one last look at her, smiled, and quietly left the way he had come, out through the front door, to where Suellyn was waiting for him patiently in her car. It was five-fifteen.

Chapter Twenty-Six

Suellyn and Jock Kelly stood silently next to each other in the basement car park. Daniel French was standing next to the police truck, hunched over, looking down at the ground and talking into the radio as William was carefully loaded into the ambulance. Suellyn blew her husband a kiss and gave him a short, pathetic wave. William rolled over and she missed the look in his eyes as he turned his head away from her.

'I'll be right behind you, William. I'll see you at the hospital.' The rear doors of the ambulance slammed shut in her face. Suellyn didn't follow the ambulance to the hospital, instead she walked over to bay sixteen where the Porsche was parked and drove out onto Marine Parade, turned into the first street on the right, locked the steering wheel hard and executed a perfect three point turn. She was heading back towards the city.

In a junior suite on the tenth floor of the Barclay Hotel, Tommy Dwyer was lying on top of the covers of an unmade king-sized bed drinking black coffee and eating toast. 'Sunrise,' a television news service was screening on the plasma screen bolted to the wall opposite the bed. He was lying low in the city hotel trying to fill his time by sleeping, watching television and ordering room service until the money from the sale of his beach house and the inheritance from Rose Phillips's estate hit his bank account.

A knock on the door startled him. He rolled off the bed. In the hallway, the morning newspaper was neatly folded and propped up against the wall next to the door. Suellyn bent down and picked it up just as the door opened. She looked up at Tommy. He was standing in the doorway, his clenched fists resting on his hips. The fluffy white hotel dressing gown he was wearing was open, exposing his chest which was covered in a mass of tight, springy, grey hairs.

'Well, look who's here. Hello stranger,' Tommy said.

Suellyn breezed past him without saying a word and slapped the newspaper against his chest. 'Well, that's a nice hello.'

Suellyn didn't seem to notice the sarcasm in his voice. 'William's in Manly Private Hospital. He was trapped in the steam room at our apartment block last night. I don't suppose you'd know anything about that would you, Tommy?'

Tommy Dwyer stared at Suellyn with a blank look on his face. He was good at disguising his emotions, perhaps too good. Suellyn sat down on the bed and took a bite of his cold toast.

'After you dropped me home last night, I was so drunk I didn't even think to wonder where William was. I thought he must have been working late when I woke up this morning and he wasn't in the apartment. The building superintendent found him when he was doing his rounds and called an ambulance. You might be interested to know that the police are asking questions and I get the impression that they don't think it was an accident. I heard them asking the super about the automatic safety switch.'

'Poor William,' Tommy muttered, without attempting to hide his sarcasm. 'He's certainly having a rough time of it lately. Is he going to be all right? Maintenance in some of these high rise apartment buildings isn't always as it should be.'

'Yeah, right, I bet you're sorry, Tommy, real sorry. Where were you last night anyway? Got an alibi for where you were after you left me?'

'When did you start playing cops and robbers? And why are you suddenly so concerned about William?' Tommy sat next to Suellyn on the bed, placed his arm around her shoulder and spoke to her softly. 'It was just going to be you and me from now on, remember Sues? The settlement money from the sale of the beach house should be through either today or tomorrow and the probate from Rose's estate will be finalised by the end of the week, or so Bartholomew says. You said that St John woman had a buyer for it. Once all the money starts to flow in we can take off to anywhere you want, Paris, the Caribbean, you name it – just you and me. We can go anywhere; do anything we want for the rest of our lives. Isn't that what you've always wanted? We could even have a baby if that's important to you.'

Suellyn realised what Tommy was saying was

true. No more sitting around at home waiting for William to turn up when he felt like it. But now things had changed and there were the letters to consider. William almost died last night and if he had died, all the obstacles to marrying Tommy would have disappeared. No messy divorce, no lawyers, no arguments. Wasn't it Tommy she loved? He was the only man who had ever made any attempt to understand her and her moods, and to put up with them. They thought alike, they understood each other, he was always around for her. But Suellyn couldn't believe she was thinking like this, there was no way she was going to back off. She needed answers from Tommy, and she needed them now.

There was something nagging Suellyn, a niggling, uneasy feeling that Tommy Dwyer wasn't really the man she thought he was. The letters had thrown up a whole lot of doubt in her mind and those doubts were taking her to all sorts of places she didn't really want to go. Had he only been using her to get to Rose and William? Well, if he had, she had already decided that two could play at his game. These letters she found were valuable, worth something to Tommy, maybe worth his share of the inheritance. Suellyn knew she had to tackle Tommy head on, once and for all and now was the time to do it.

'Tommy...' but before Suellyn could say anything, Tommy had her in his arms. She felt the brush of his tongue against hers as it played gently inside her mouth. He pressed his body hard up against hers, but she didn't want this, not now when she was so confused about her feelings for him. She dug her fingernails into his arm, their teeth gnashed against each other as she pulled away from his embrace.

'Stop it Tommy!' She screamed.

'Stop what? What's wrong now?'

'There's something I have to ask you. I need to know the truth. You have to tell me.'

'For God's sake. Tell you what? What have you got your self worked up about now woman?' Tommy's patience was wearing thin.

'It's about the letters.'

'What letters? What are you talking about?'

'You know what I'm talking about. A carbon copy of a letter I found at the beach house. It was in a cardboard box in the back of your wardrobe. I found the original letter at Rose's house. She had it hidden behind one of William's baby photos in a photo frame next to her bed; the letter was from your mother and dated only a few weeks before she died.'

Tommy looked at Suellyn.

'And there's this threatening letter you wrote to your mother.'

He knew what was coming next and he thought it was a pity, a real shame. He liked Suellyn Phillips but nothing was going to get in the way of his plans. He thought he had this all worked out, but he had thought wrong. He had underestimated her. He didn't realise that she had a conscience. 'Well go on Suellyn, get what's troubling you off your chest.'

'Tommy, tell me, did you kill your mother? Did you kill Rose? Did you try to kill William?' Suellyn stood up from the bed and studied his eyes, trying to find the truth that lay hidden behind them. 'Did you only pretend to love me to get to my family?'

'What sort of question is that?'

'The only one I have for you,' Suellyn shot back. She didn't wait for Tommy to answer her. 'It's over Tommy. I know what you've done.'

Tommy stood up and circled her. He placed his hands gently around the graceful curve of her slender neck, pulled back her jumper and kissed the top of her shoulders lightly and tenderly. He had hoped it wouldn't come to this, but there was no other way. Nobody would miss her if she suddenly disappeared, he knew that. People go missing all the time, especially women like Suellyn Phillips.

Suellyn reached behind her and put her slender fingers on top of his. She tried to pry them away from her neck. She was surprised by his strength. When he pressed the tips of his fingers deep into the side of her neck, Suellyn's survival instincts kicked in, she began to fight. Tommy responded. He placed his hand over her mouth, but she freed herself from his grip. She swung her arms around wildly and kicked her heels hard into his shins. He released his grip momentarily and she transferred all her weight onto her right foot so that she could balance herself. He was like a madman, he came at her repeatedly, grabbed her around the waist as she tried to reach the front door. Instinctively, Suellyn's body dipped to one side to avoid him, but he executed a well-timed rugby tackle. He reached out and grabbed her calves and dragged her body back to him like a crazed animal. He rolled her over onto her back, belly up and mounted her. The look on Suellyn's face as she stared into Tommy's dark eyes was one of sheer terror. He flattened the weight of his body against her and again he tightened his grip around her neck. They struggled on the floor; his face contorted and turned red with the effort of restraining her. It was at that point that Suellyn Phillips decided it was time to scream, there wasn't anything else she could think of to do. The scream was more like a howl, the sound of a bitch in heat. He responded instantly to her outburst by placing his hand hard over her mouth. Their bodies moved together, she bucked him and he pressed down on her more heavily this time - his eyes wide, stared into hers and she waited, expecting the inevitable, a swift ending. He knew her body well enough to be able to anticipate her every move. He wedged one of his knees into her stomach, pinning her securely to the floor. Her eyes bulged and the blood drained from her face. An explosion of bright lights went off in her head like a box of Chinese fire crackers. She didn't want to die. She tried to shift her weight from underneath him but he weighed at least thirty kilos more than she did and as her body trembled, she wanted to shout, to scream, to do anything to stop him, but the restriction on her larynx stopped her from uttering a single word.

A loud knock at the door startled both of them. The distraction was enough that Tommy's hand slipped from Suellyn's mouth. He hesitated as he turned his head in the direction of the door. Suellyn gasped for air and kicked and clawed at him with the last ounce of strength she had left, red welts formed on his cheek as her long tapered nails clawed at him; they wrestled, their bodies became as one as they rolled across the floor. Suellyn lashed out at him with her long bare legs, with her skirt riding up her thighs she struck out at him and knocked the corner of the glass coffee table next to the lounge, sending an expensive looking Chinese lamp exploding to the tiled floor.

Rimis drew his Glock 22 from his leather holster inside his jacket, turned the door handle hard and pushed his shoulder against the unlocked door while Brennan crouched down low and rushed into the room behind him.

Two burly police officers cuffed Tommy Dwyer and cautioned him. He was dragged to his feet and led away with his arms firmly secured behind his back. Brennan stepped back from the doorway and raised her eyebrows as Tommy passed her. She almost felt sorry for him as she noticed the scratches on the side of his face and realised that he had probably bitten off more than he could chew when he took on Suellyn Phillips.

Rather than take the lift and run the risk of a chance meeting with a member of the public, Tommy Dwyer was escorted to the basement car park by the fire stairs and was led out through the ground floor fire exit doors. He was dragged down the ten flights of stairs with his head bowed, his shoulders slumped - looking more than his sixty-four years. Apart from the scratches to his cheek, Suellyn had also delivered to her attacker some rather nasty claw marks to his upper chest and two large distinctive bite marks circled his bruised nipples. The man looked like he had been attacked by a wild animal.

Nick Rimis handed Suellyn a glass of water. She ignored him and the glass. He thought to himself that the woman had guts, despite her bad temper and crazy mood swings. He looked at her sitting on the lounge with her feet tucked beneath her. She looked vulnerable and childlike and something stirred in Rimis, an overwhelming feeling that he needed to protect this woman. Someone had thought to throw a blanket around her shoulders and as she sat on the lounge in a state of shock, Rimis wished that he had insisted they call an ambulance.

'Suellyn,' he muttered her name gently, trying to reconnect with her and bring her back to the real world.'

Suellyn looked up at him with red brimmed and swollen eyes.

'Are you sure you wouldn't like us to call an ambulance?' he asked with genuine concern in his voice. She had been through hell and back with Tommy Dwyer. The red marks and bruises on her neck were a testament to that. It was only by chance that he and Brennan showed up when they did. If they'd arrived any later, it was anyone's guess as to what would have happened next.

Suellyn looked at the good looking detective

standing in front of her. Wasn't this the macho guy who only yesterday accused her of murdering her mother-in-law? Here he was again, standing in a city hotel room after having saved her life. Tommy Dwyer, she realised would have killed her, or at least, given it a damn good try. 'No, I'm okay,' she whispered hoarsely. She spread her fingers lightly over her thin delicate throat. 'My throat hurts like hell and my body doesn't feel much better, but I think I'll survive.' She smiled weakly as she looked into Rimis's deep, brown eyes.

As he looked back at her, he realised there was something about this woman, something special. He was surprised that she was able to manage a smile after all she had been through and he wondered what was going to happen to Suellyn Phillips. She had lied to him about her whereabouts on the day Rose Phillips was murdered but now wasn't the time to talk about that.

'We'll organise a car to take you home. Is there anyone we can call for you, a close friend, a relative?' Rimis asked.

'No, there's nobody really, thanks all the same, but I'm fine. I really am. I think I'll just take some paracetamol and go to bed when I get home. I promise I'll call my GP tomorrow. But there is one thing you could do for me.'

'Name it.'

'Tell William what happened,' she turned and looked at the female detective standing next to him. 'Tell him… tell him that I'm sorry. I'm sorry for everything.'

Chapter Twenty-Seven

The early light of day entered the hospital room. The night shift had just finished and a tea trolley rattled up the corridor; lights were switched on and a young intern was conducting her early morning rounds. It was another day, a day William Phillips had never expected to see. As he lay in his bed, propped up with the help of two plump pillows, he looked out through his private hospital room window at a cold, drizzly day and hoped that the new shift would be more sympathetic to his needs and a lot younger and prettier than the previous lot.

A new face entered his room.

'Good morning William.'

He could tell by her accent, her green eyes and her thick, short cropped raven hair that Catherine was Irish. She flipped over a page on his medical chart and pulled the trolley with all the gizmos on it over to his hospital bed and began the tedious task of measuring and monitoring his blood pressure, temperature and heart rate. Catherine popped a thermometer under his tongue and held his wrist.

William was relieved when he was told by the emergency registrar, that he'd not suffered a heart attack. What he had experienced in the steam room was an anxiety attack, dehydration, hyperventilation and physical stress caused by extreme temperature, not to mention the concussion he sustained when he collapsed and fell to the floor.

'So, how are you this morning, William?' Catherine said in her fine Irish brogue.' Feel better for a good night's sleep?'

'A lot better thanks. At least a lot better than I did this time yesterday morning, to be sure, to be sure.'

She laughed politely at his corny attempt to impersonate her accent. She recorded his blood pressure and wondered why it was that patients always thought they could imitate Irish accents and why they even bothered. After arriving in Australia every second person she met had an Irish ancestor sitting somewhere on a branch in their family tree. At first she thought it was a clever pickup line, but then soon realised as she got to know a few Australian larrikins that there were many similarities between these Aussie males and the lads she had left behind in Wexford.

Catherine left the room and William returned to his cup of coffee. He was unwrapping a packet of plain sweet biscuits when Jill Brennan tapped lightly on the open door to his private hospital room. His hair was ruffled after sleep and he needed a shave. A business show on the television was quietly running in the background and a copy of *The Australian* and *The Financial Review* were lying open across his knees. His mobile phone was resting on his stomach.

'Don't you ever sleep?'

Jill smiled at his remark and realised she wasn't the only one to take her job seriously. 'And don't you ever relax?' she said, as she stared at the financial papers in his lap.

William looked at the papers and dropped them to the floor. He turned off the television, switched off his phone and placed it inside the top drawer of his bedside table.

'How are you William, I was just on my way home to have breakfast. It's been one of those nights. But you're looking a lot brighter than what I expected. Constable French filled me in on what happened last night.'

'I feel a lot better. I'll probably be out of here tomorrow.'

'That's good news,' she said.

'Pull up a chair.' William indicated to the chair tucked in a corner of the room. 'Like a biscuit?'

Jill smiled and shook her head. She dragged the grey vinyl armchair up to the side of the bed, sat down next to him and took out her note book and pen from her shoulder bag.

'That looks official,' William said, as he looked at the note book in her lap and took a bite of the biscuit.

'Oh, sorry, force of habit,' she said as she returned the notepad to her bag. 'William, I've got some more bad news to tell you, I'm afraid.'

The blood from William's face drained. 'What's happened now? It seems that every time I see you, you've got bad news to tell me.' He couldn't imagine that things could get much worse. A timely knock at the door allowed William a moment to prepare himself for whatever it was he was about to hear from Jill Brennan. They both watched as a young male orderly entered the room and collected William's completed menu sheet. The orderly placed a bottle of spring water on his bedside table and left. William moved the table tray to one side and hoisted himself into a comfortable position so he was sitting upright. He locked onto Jill's eyes. 'Well go on then, tell me. What's happened now?'

Jill looked back at William and remembered the first day she met him. He looked so different now, a lot softer, more vulnerable somehow. 'We've arrested Tommy Dwyer on two counts of attempted murder and two counts of murder.'

William looked at Jill, puzzled.

'Rose, and Isabelle Dwyer. He's confessed to everything,' she said. Jill waited for William to say something, but he just stared at her. He didn't say a word. He was processing the information, his biscuit fell from his hand into his coffee cup, dissolving and disappearing without a trace.

'But you said two attempted murders?' William was confused. 'So he tried to kill me right? But who...?'

'Suellyn,' Brennan said simply.

William raised his eyebrows in disbelief and held the bridge of his nose between his thumb and index finger and massaged his nose gently. 'What happened?'

'Your wife went to the hotel where Tommy Dwyer was staying and confronted him. She asked him about the contents of the letter his mother had written to Rose. It appears he realised that it was no use lying to her anymore when she accused him of murdering both his mother and Rose and also trying to murder you. When we questioned him, he told us that he planned to marry Suellyn after he killed you. That way he would get his hands on both inheritances at the same time, but Suellyn became suspicious and began to suspect him of murdering Isabelle and Rose and trying to murder you. He knew he couldn't trust her to keep her mouth shut and that's when he decided to kill her. I suppose he thought he had already killed two women, another one wouldn't make any difference. At that point he thought he could still work his way out of the corner he had backed himself into. If he killed Suellyn, disposed of her body with the idea that nobody would really miss her, when questioned over the matter of the incident in the steam room, he was going to point the finger in Suellyn's direction because he was sure there was no evidence to incriminate him. Dead men or in this case, dead women tell no tales. She was the scapegoat if you like. With you and Suellyn both out of the way, your share of Rose's inheritance would go to him. We don't know if he had plans to get rid of the other beneficiary, Kevin Taggart.'

Jill looked at William.

William didn't say a word. He took a long, deep mouthful of coffee and closed his eyes.

Chapter Twenty-Eight

A buff coloured envelope arrived from the solicitor in the morning post. It was addressed to Mr Kevin Taggart.

Kevin ripped the envelope open. With wild eyes he scanned the letter from Martin Bartholomew and after reading the contents, he let the A4 page fall from his hands, watching it as it landed gently on the kitchen table. He bent over and picked up the envelope which had fallen onto the floor, looked inside and pulled out the cheque, studying it closely. The texture and the amount written on the cheque made his heart beat faster and his hands tremble. He held it tightly, close to his face and breathed deeply as if he could smell his newly acquired wealth. When he released his breath which he had been holding, he extended his arms in front of him and screamed a jubilant scream at the top of his voice. After regaining his composure, his breathing returned to normal and he found himself looking at the cheque. He studied it for some time and became entranced by the thick dollar sign and the sturdy strokes of Mr Bartholomew's handwriting. He was captivated by the roundness of the three and the symmetry of the five zeros which followed it. The comma separating the digits resembled a tadpole - its tail casually dropping below the thin printed line, the punctuation mark delineated the numbers and emphasized the cheque's value. Then the spell was broken. Kevin scavenged through the cutlery drawer in search of a fridge magnet; a souvenir from a day trip to a Reptile Park on the Central Coast. He attached the magnet to the cheque and placed it on the fridge. Then he took a step back from it and admired it in the same way he would a piece of art.

'Good old Rose, I knew she would come through for me. After all, that's what good neighbours are for,' he laughed hysterically.

Kevin decided a celebration was called for, but there was no one he could think of that he wanted to share his good fortune with. He opened the fridge door and grabbed a bottle of full strength beer. 'Here's to you Mother dear, what a shame you aren't here to share in my good fortune.' Kevin twisted the screw cap, lifted it to his lips and threw back a large mouthful of the icy cold brew. He swallowed hard. With the bottle of beer still in his hand, Kevin returned to his studio and tuned into his favourite station. He listened to the classical music playing. The uplifting music settled him and he reached into his paint box and selected a tube of red acrylic paint and immediately concentrated on the blank canvas sitting on the easel before him. He circled the easel slowly, just as a predator would who was studying its prey before pouncing, looking at it from different angles, deciding where he should place the first stroke. The starkness of the white canvas beckoned him and finally he found the courage to begin. He took a deep breath, dabbed at the paint on the palette and made the first brush stroke. The sable brush glided over the canvas. A narrow, soft ray of autumn sunshine hit the window and Kevin realised how happy and how extremely grateful he was for the bounties which had been bestowed upon him.

He recited Cicero. 'A thankful heart is not only the greatest virtue, but the parent of all the other virtues.'

The weather was deteriorating. Kevin stood at the window with his paint brush in his hand and looked up at the darkening sky. A line of heavy clouds filed in from the west and extinguished the remaining light. To continue painting was impossible.

A torn *Chesty Bonds* singlet splattered with a kaleidoscope of colours lay draped on the table where Kevin stored his brushes, crayons and lead pencils. He dipped his brush in a jar of clean water and wiped it dry. Time for lunch. His stomach demanded food and he walked up the hall into the kitchen.

Lunch was a slice of wholemeal toast on a stark white round dinner plate swamped with a can of cold baked beans. Kevin looked down at his plate and imagined a more sumptuous fare. Perhaps grilled Tasmanian salmon with a light salad and polenta chips on the side. Kevin Taggart had a feeling that things were about to change in his life, he had a feeling in his bones. He devoured the baked beans and the soggy toast and began to make a mental list of the things he wanted do with his windfall. A holiday first he thought, an extended tour of the Tuscan hill towns and then perhaps a side trip to Florence to paint the clay roofs and of course, a visit to the Uffizi Gallery. He might even take a Mediterranean cruise.

The house was quiet. Seated on a vinyl chair at his kitchen table he began to daydream. He looked critically at the outdated kitchen. It had never bothered him before, but now that he had some money to spend, he realised how drab and out of fashion it had become. It needed renovating; the once white paint on the kitchen cupboards and drawers had yellowed with age. The paint was peeling. The small rectangular 'mission brown' tiles on the splashbacks were a mistake of the seventies. They looked dull and dirty after years of accumulated grime. The open timber shelves on the kitchen wall displayed his late mother's best crockery set or at least the pieces that had survived the service of the years. A rusty nail on the side of the shelves held his house and car keys. A handy location when he was in a hurry to leave the house.

A loud thump and the sound of metal scraping against concrete brought Kevin to his feet. He walked towards the front of the house and entered his bedroom. Dirty, grey crumpled sheets lay at the foot of his bed. A pile of art books lay scattered on the floor under the window. He stepped over them and looked out between the slats of the rusty venetian blinds. He opened a row with his thumb and index finger and roughly wiped away years of accumulated dust as he looked out at the scene across the street.

Three solidly built Maoris were loading the contents of the house into a beaten-up, bottle green removalist truck which was parked in front of the

Blake house. 'Three Men and a Green Truck' was spray painted in white lettering on the side of the truck and a tall, slim, middle aged man stood beside it, calling instructions to the three men. He was wearing a pair of beige cotton chinos and a yellow polo shirt. A New York Yankees baseball cap was perched on the top of his head to shade his eyes from the sun. A relative, a nephew perhaps? He was too well dressed to be from the removalist company, Kevin thought.

A procession of furniture trailed out from the house. Rhoda's prized carved timber sideboard was rolled down the front steps on a trolley and came to rest on the footpath along with the fridge, the microwave oven and the boxes of household items. Kevin recognised his painting, *North Coast Summers*. It was leaning up against the gum tree in front of the house and he decided he would contact Mr Martin Bartholomew, the executor of *the sisters'* estates, and ask for it back. The youngest and fittest looking of the trio, scratched his head as he considered how best to pack the truck.

Kevin looked at the women's possessions parked on the footpath and a rush of sentiment descended upon him. He watched two of the men carry out the red, lumpy lounge by its ends, and walk it up the metal plank at the rear of the truck. He remembered the afternoons and evenings he had spent sitting on the lounge and the smell and taste of cheap sherry sprang to mind. The matching red chairs were loaded next and carried by the shortest of the three men, whose thick biceps were covered in dark blue traditional Maori tattoos.

Kevin stood behind the Venetian slats observing the scene for some time before deciding a better view was to be had outside. He walked down the hallway past the kitchen and out through the back door, down the concrete steps to where he kept his gardening equipment in a galvanized steel tool box. He picked out a pair of garden clippers and walked up the driveway to the front fence. As the blades chomped into the overgrown Moraya hedge, he looked across at the men who had now stopped work for lunch. They were sitting under the gum tree, with a large eski propped open, they were drinking beer from cans, eating home made sandwiches made from thick bread and laughing, obviously relaxed in each other's company. The well dressed man had left and Kevin observed that his painting was nowhere to be seen. It had already been loaded onto the truck.

After lunch was eaten and the last of the cardboard boxes was loaded, Kevin watched the three men as they packed themselves into the front seat of the truck. The blare of country and western music from the local radio station, and the grating of the gears as they changed from first to second and then to third, trailed behind the truck as it lumbered up Eden Street. He wondered where *the sisters'* possessions were being taken and what was to become of them. He hoped his painting wouldn't end up in a charity store or on a rubbish tip. He would explain to Mr Bartholomew that the painting was his and that he would like it returned. He would ask him who he should speak to.

Kevin assumed that the house had been sold even though a 'For Sale' sign had not appeared at the front of the house. After the interest which had been shown in Rose's house, he wouldn't be surprised if a disappointed potential buyer had been rewarded for their patience by the sudden listing of the brick bungalow across the street.

Kevin returned inside, sat down at the kitchen table and contemplated the value of the Blake sisters' estate. He took a deep and satisfied breath and tried to control his excitement as he looked forward to the arrival of another letter, and another cheque, from Mr Martin Bartholomew.

Chapter Twenty-Nine

Kevin Taggart stood with his arms crossed in front of his chest watching the small crowd of art lovers admiring his work. Another champagne cork hit the ceiling and Jill Brennan's shrill laugh bounced off the walls and crossed the room to where he was standing in a corner by himself.

'Here's to Kevin,' Jill raised her champagne flute in his direction and smiled.

Kevin looked down at the floor and studied his feet. He wasn't enjoying this as much as he thought he would. But he couldn't disguise the pride he felt as he looked at his art on the broad white walls of the gallery which was located in a busy, tree lined street in a trendy part of the eastern suburbs. The crowd had started arriving half an hour earlier and the response had been more than he and Jill had hoped for.

Suellyn Phillips also raised her glass to Kevin and smiled at him from across the opposite side of the room. The plunging neckline of her above the knee black cocktail dress revealed a round and firm cleav-

241

age. She was holding a catalogue in one hand and a glass of bubbly in the other. She stood in front of his painting, *The Red Lounge* and leaned forward to study the brush strokes in an attempt to unravel the secrets of his techniques.

Rimis had a beer in his hand and walked up behind Kevin and slapped him hard on the back.

'Congratulations Kevin old son. I hope there aren't any bad feelings. Just doing my job you know.'

'No hard feelings, Detective Senior Sergeant. I do realise that you were only doing your job and I hope you now realise that I was only doing what I thought was my job? That was to take care of the elderly people in Eden Street.'

Rimis smiled. He really had thought Kevin had murdered the Blake sisters but there was no evidence to prove it. What quality of life did they have anyway? The younger sister, Edi Blake was practically non compus-mentis. But Kevin did all right out of it. Managed to score another three hundred grand from *the sisters* and got his painting back. He looked over at *North Coast Summers.* It held pride of place on an easel in the middle of the room.

When he entered the painting in the Wynne Prize, Kevin never imagined in his wildest dreams that he had a chance of winning the coveted award. *North Coast Summers* was recognised by a panel of judges to be the best landscape painting of Australian scenery in watercolours by an Australian artist. Winning the prize which had a dollar value of twenty-five thousand dollars attached to it, catapulted Kevin into the heady and exciting art world with all its snobbery and pretension.

Rimis walked up to Jill and planted a kiss on her left cheek. He looked across at Kevin who was discussing a painting with an interested buyer and Jill followed his eyes as Rimis leant into her. Without taking his eye off Kevin, he said in a deep whisper, 'I might not know much about art Brennan, but I know a villain when I see one.'

Rimis adjusted his tie. 'Hope you made the right decision. Why you decided to give up the world of crime for this, I never could figure,' he said a little too loudly. He looked at the people milling around in small groups, sipping champagne and pretending to know what good art looked like.

'I know I did.' She winked at him and excused herself when she saw William talking with Ashleigh Taylor.

Rimis looked around the room searching for Suellyn Phillips. He loved the dress. He decided she wasn't as stuck up and neurotic as he first thought. There was a lot to admire about Suellyn Phillips. She had been brave to take on Tommy Dwyer and Rimis noticed that she was becoming the life of the party. Since he had been watching her, she had thrown back three glasses of French champagne.

As soon as he walked through the front door of the gallery, William searched the crowd for Jill. When he spotted her she was talking with her old boss and he decided he would wait for her to approach him, rather than interrupt her.

He had his back to her now and was looking through the catalogue with Ashleigh Taylor. Jill walked up to him and placed her hand gently on the sleeve of his cashmere jumper and noticed that it brought out the colour of his eyes when he turned around and looked at her. 'Hello William. I'm glad you could come. It's been a long time.'

'Wouldn't have missed it for the world.'

'Hello Doctor Taylor. I hope you're enjoying the exhibition?' Jill Brennan asked.

'I am, thanks. Excuse me will you? I want to go and speak to Kevin while he's free.'

William Phillips stared into Jill's eyes and felt a stirring of emotion. God, she was beautiful. Now that his divorce from Suellyn was Decree Absolute he was planning to see a lot more of Jill Brennan. Perhaps they even had a future together. He hoped so. They had a lot in common.

Jill brushed her blonde hair back from her face and wondered what he was thinking. William Phillips was an attractive man in so many ways, but he had suffered enough. If he gave her the chance, she would promise him one thing, there would be no more secrets, no more lies.

'Here's to Rose Phillips,' Kevin lifted his glass and threw back the fizzy contents of the champagne flute. He had never tasted champagne before, but he thought he could acquire a taste for it.

'To Rose Phillips!' the small crowd chorused as they lifted their glasses in the air even though half the people there had no idea who Rose Phillips was.

'And here's to Rhoda and Edi Blake, let's not forget them. May they also rest in eternal peace,' Kevin raised his glass again.

Kevin had already noticed the small, round red stickers on some of his paintings and Jill Brennan was buzzing around the gallery looking very pleased with herself.

Kevin walked up to William Phillips and looked him straight in the eye. 'If it wasn't for your mother, I wouldn't be here today,' he said quietly.

'If it wasn't for my mother, I wouldn't be who I am today,' William replied.

Acknowledgements

I would like to thank those who read later drafts of this book and offered support and constructive criticism: Kerry-Ann Aitken, Roslyn Diesner, Zoe Trussell, Alex Trussell and Julie Terrason.

Thank you to Rachel Terrason for her invaluable assistance with police procedure and terminology.

Thanks to Caroline Webber from Green Olive Press for her editorial services and her understanding of what it feels like to let go of a manuscript.

And a special thank you to my husband, Mark, whose blind belief in my ability and his technical support helped me achieve my dream.